Ken Ludwig's
Baskerville:

A Sherlock Holmes Mystery

SAMUELFRENCH.COM   SAMUELFRENCH.CO.UK

ISBN 978-0-573-70419-2

www.SamuelFrench.com
www.SamuelFrench.co.uk

FOR PRODUCTION ENQUIRIES
UNITED STATES AND CANADA
Info@SamuelFrench.com
1-866-598-8449
UNITED KINGDOM AND EUROPE
Plays@SamuelFrench.co.uk
020-7255-4302

Each title is subject to availability from Samuel French, depending
upon country of performance. Please be aware that *KEN LUDWIG'S
BASKERVILLE: A SHERLOCK HOLMES MYSTERY* may not be licensed
by Samuel French in your territory. Professional and amateur producers
should contact the nearest Samuel French office or licensing partner to
verify availability.

system, or transmitted in any form, by any means, now known or yet to be invented, including mechanical, electronic, photocopying, recording, videotaping, or otherwise, without the prior written permission of the publisher. No one shall upload this title(s), or part of this title(s), to any social media websites.

For all enquiries regarding motion picture, television, and other media rights, please contact Samuel French.

MUSIC USE NOTE

Licensees are solely responsible for obtaining formal written permission from copyright owners to use copyrighted music in the performance of this play and are strongly cautioned to do so. If no such permission is obtained by the licensee, then the licensee must use only original music that the licensee owns and controls. Licensees are solely responsible and liable for all music clearances and shall indemnify the copyright owners of the play(s) and their licensing agent, Samuel French, against any costs, expenses, losses and liabilities arising from the use of music by licensees. Please contact the appropriate music licensing authority in your territory for the rights to any incidental music.

IMPORTANT BILLING AND CREDIT REQUIREMENTS

If you have obtained performance rights to this title, please refer to your licensing agreement for important billing and credit requirements.

KEN LUDWIG'S BASKERVILLE: A SHERLOCK HOLMES MYSTERY was first produced as a co-production between McCarter Theatre Center for the Performing Arts (Emily Mann, Artistic Director; Timothy J. Shields, Managing Director) and Arena Stage (Molly Smith, Artistic Director; Edgar Dobie, Executive Director) at Arena Stage's Kreeger Theater in Washington, D.C. The opening night was January 16, 2015. Following the run at Arena Stage, the production subsequently shifted to the McCarter Theatre Center's Matthews Theatre in Princeton, New Jersey. The opening night was March 13, 2015. The performance was directed by Amanda Dehnert, with sets by Daniel Ostling, costumes by Jess Goldstein, lights by Philip Rosenberg, and sound by Joshua Horvath and Raymond Nardelli. The Production Stage Manager was Alison Cote. The Assistant Stage Manager was Kurt Hall. The cast was as follows:

SHERLOCK HOLMES	Gregory Wooddell
DOCTOR WATSON	Lucas Hall
ACTOR 1	Stanley Bahorek
ACTOR 2	Michael Glenn
ACTRESS 1	Jane Pfitsch

KEN LUDWIG'S BASKERVILLE: A SHERLOCK HOLMES MYSTERY was subsequently produced by The Old Globe (Barry Edelstein, Artistic Director; Michael G. Murphy, Managing Director) in San Diego, California. The opening night was July 30, 2015. The performance was directed by Josh Rhodes, with sets by Wilson Chin, costumes by Shirley Pierson, lights by Austin R. Smith, and original music and sound by Bart Fasbender. The Production Stage Manager was Annette Yé. The cast was as follows:

SHERLOCK HOLMES	Euan Morton
DOCTOR WATSON	Usman Ally
ACTOR 1	Blake Segal
ACTOR 2	Andrew Kober
ACTRESS 1	Liz Wisan

CHARACTERS

Sherlock Holmes
Doctor Watson

Actor One	Actor Two	Actress One
Dr. Mortimer	Sir Charles	Mrs. Hudson
Baron Scarpia	Baskerville	Maiden
Man with Black Beard	Daisy	Shepherdess
Lucy	Sir Hugo Baskerville	Floria Tosca
Milker	Bradley the Tobacconist	Cartwright
Castilian Desk Clerk		German Maid
Train Conductor	Sir Henry Baskerville	Baby
Trap Driver	Wilson	Mrs. Clayton
Barrymore	Inspector Lestrade	Mrs. Barrymore
Stapleton		Miss Stapleton
Victor		Nurse Malloy
Doctor McCann		Winnie
Country Farmer		Nurse MacKeeble
Sir John Falstaff		Laura Lyons

SETTING

London & Devonshire

TIME

The late 1890s

The Romance of Sherlock Holmes:
A Q&A with Ken Ludwig

Ken Ludwig and Linda Lombardi, Literary Director at Arena Stage in Washington, D.C., discussed Baskerville: A Sherlock Holmes Mystery *as part of the Arena Stage/McCarter Theatre Center co-production. This interview was originally published on January 22, 2015 on* Stage Banter: the Arena Stage Blog.

What is it that makes Sherlock Holmes and Dr. Watson so popular with both writers and audiences?

There is something romantic at the heart of Sherlock Holmes that touches all of us. He is quixotic, cerebral, dashing and inspiring. But there is also something dark and dangerous about Holmes, and we admire him for the courage with which he fights his demons. He broods, he plays Beethoven, he revels in danger and experiments with drugs. At times he frightens us, and that is part of his allure.

Meanwhile, Watson creates a resonance of his own. He is steady, stalwart and wonderfully earthbound. Together they are Don Quixote and Sancho Panza. They are Ariel and Caliban. They are fire and earth. These roots plant them firmly in our shared mythology, and we respond to them as we respond to all mythological characters, not just through the brain, but also viscerally and through our hearts.

Sherlock Holmes is one of the most famous characters to be portrayed in literature, in film and on TV. What attracted you to him and, in particular, *The Hound of the Baskervilles?*

Sherlock Holmes and Doctor Watson have been a staple of our culture since the 1890s, but they have recently re-entered our world in a more muscular way. For some reason, it seems to be just the right time for Holmes and Watson. Perhaps these days we crave a hero who succeeds despite, or perhaps because of his quirks, his obsessions and his near-fatal flaws.

Also, it is easy to dismiss Sir Arthur Conan Doyle as a writer of mere genre literature. After all, say the critics, he wrote only mysteries and adventure stories. But the man had a touch of genius about him. Certainly his genius was different in kind from that of, say, Jane Austen or Henry James. It was not as deeply personal or psychological. But genius comes in many shapes, and Conan Doyle inhabited one of them.

To begin with, he virtually invented the entire mystery genre as we know it. There would be no Agatha Christie without Conan Doyle, no

Dorothy Sayers, no Raymond Chandler, and no detective movies or television shows. The detective and his sidekick, the locked-room mystery, the clues, the red herrings, the bungling policeman and the grateful client – he virtually invented all of it.

In addition, in the characters of Holmes and Watson, he somehow plumbed the depths of our immortal souls – and his audience recognized this from the beginning. Think about the number of times in the history of literature that there have been people literally waiting in line for a novel or story. I can think of Charles Dickens; I can think of J.K. Rowling; and I can think of Conan Doyle, whose myriad fans would wait on the dock in New York for the latest installment of Sherlock Holmes in *The Strand Magazine*. The public realized instantly that Holmes and Watson were not just for an age but for all time.

As for *The Hound of the Baskervilles*, Conan Doyle wrote it with his usual instinct for a whopping good story. Again, in the history of English literature, how many truly great adventure stories have been written –stories of depth and quality that create mythologies and yet keep you turning the pages while you hold your breath. I would include *Treasure Island* and *The Hobbit. Kidnapped*, perhaps, and *The Prisoner of Zenda*. And preeminent among them is *The Hound of the Baskervilles*. Like *Treasure Island*, it contains a villain who reaches deeply into our subconscious. And like *Treasure Island*, it touches on the darkness in all of us. The very image of the hound brings out the danger that lurks in the depths of our souls. The hound is mysterious and unknowable, and so are we. He is frightening and difficult to control. There is a hound in all of us.

Why write a play about Sherlock Holmes at this moment in time?

There is a great tradition of melodrama in our theater, both English and American. In melodramas, we sit on the edge of our seats watching exciting stories where anything can happen. There are villains, there are mysteries, there are fortunes lost and reputations regained. These are the plays that defined our theater for over two hundred years, and the literary icons we most revere, like Jane Austen and Charles Dickens, loved to act in them and write about them.

There should be a bigger place in our lives for these kinds of plays. They needn't be a steady diet, but they shouldn't disappear, either. Beginning in the 1930s, this genre was subsumed by Hollywood movies, and the theater was poorer for it. And while I yield to no one in my love for Errol Flynn in *Robin Hood* and Kirk Douglas in *Spartacus*, I think that adventure stories are just as good, and maybe even better, when they're presented on a live stage with actors you can touch.

My hope is that *Baskerville* is about the theater as much as it is about Sherlock Holmes and Doctor Watson. I want it to succeed not only as a tale of fellowship and courage, but also as an adventure in itself. I'd love us to return, at least now and then, to nights at the theater when we feel the way we do in the movies watching *Indiana Jones and the Temple of Doom*: sitting breathless in the dark, mesmerized by the action, munching bags of popcorn.

Baskerville is a cast of five. Three of the actors play over 40 characters. What is that like in your development process, as far as writing these very distinct characters, knowing that one actor will be playing these ten roles, another these ten, another these ten?

Writing for this many characters in a single play felt joyous; and knowing that they'd be played by only three actors felt like a breath of fresh air. It was liberating.

Classical theater has always been filled with doubling and tripling, and it is often a source of theatrical joy. Shakespeare's company had between 12 and 15 actors in it, but his plays contain as many as 25-35 characters.

One of my favorite authors, J.B. Priestley, said something about theater that I like very much: He reminded us that when we go to the theater we feel two things at the same time. First, we see characters who tell us a story. Second, we're conscious that professional actors are playing those characters and telling the story on a small wooden stage.

When actors double, triple – and, in the case of *Baskerville*, play dozens of parts – we're reminded of this duality. Characters may die, but the actors are, reassuringly, still standing at the curtain when they take their bows. I believe that this knowledge can enrich the experience of seeing a play, and reminds us that play-going is not merely life, but life enhanced.

Are you more a Holmes or a Watson?

I think I'm a Watson but I wish I were a Holmes.

Finally, a question I ask all our playwrights...what's your favorite word?

"Fadge." In *Twelfth Night*, at the first great turning point in the play, Viola sums up the story and then asks, "How will this fadge?" meaning how will it all turn out in the end. What a simple, and simply breathtaking word.

Comedy in His Bones:
A Conversation with Playwright Ken Ludwig
On Adapting Arthur Conan Doyle's
The Hound of the Baskervilles

This interview between Ken Ludwig and Danielle Mages Amato, Literary Director/Dramaturg at The Old Globe in San Diego, discussed Baskerville: A Sherlock Holmes Mystery. *It was originally published in The Old Globe's* Performances Magazine.

Baskerville is not your first Sherlock Holmes play; you've written about the character before. Could you talk a bit about what draws you to Holmes?

In our literary history there are only a handful of writers who have created myth out of whole cloth. One of these is Arthur Conan Doyle. Through the alchemy of words on paper, Conan Doyle, almost overnight, created two of the most unforgettable characters in English literature. Part of the secret was the quality of his writing. Sentence for sentence, Conan Doyle writes with the brilliance of Dickens, he tells whopping stories that keep us on the edge of our seats. To top it all off, Conan Doyle was wonderfully prolific – especially with his two greatest characters. Holmes and Watson appear in four novels and fifty-six short stories, and we end up treasuring them, in part, because we know them so well.

What do you think makes Watson and Holmes such iconic characters?

I think in Holmes' case it may be because there had never been a character quite like him before. He's an admirable aesthete with a lightning-fast mind who lives for justice and is willing to die for it; at the same time, he's deeply dangerous, with a drug habit and a lack of interpersonal skills. These traits, taken together, create a sense of dangerous romance, and I think we respond to Holmes the way we respond to Heathcliff in Emily Bronte's *Wuthering Heights*: with envy and with awe at the mystery inside him. As for Watson, he's the good old sensible earth and clay to Holmes' fire and ice. He's Sancho Panza to Don Quixote, Caliban to Ariel, and we see ourselves in him.

Do you have a theory of why Sherlock Holmes seems to be having a cultural renaissance right now?

The darkness and danger of Sherlock Holmes that I spoke about a moment ago seem to symbolize our peculiar moment in history. Holmes is neurotic, which I think explains exactly why we're so drawn to him in these troubling times. Somehow,

Conan Doyle found the perfect character to reflect the twentieth century that lay ahead of him. At the same time, Holmes is part of a literary genre that we find particularly reassuring at the moment. In traditional mysteries (as in classic comedies) the world may seem topsy-turvy as we bump and rattle along through the bulk of the story, but by the end, it somehow rights itself. Think of a jigsaw puzzle. The writer throws all the pieces up in the air in a way that seems unsolvable; but somehow, through the magic of storytelling, all the pieces fall to earth and lock into place. This pattern gives us confidence that our lives will be all right in the end.

Why did you decide to adapt *The Hound of the Baskervilles?*

I think *Hound* is the best of all the Holmes stories. It's clever and crafty, filled with colorful characters (and an especially fine villain), has evocative settings, and it moves like lightning. Also, it's the perfect length dramatically–it's not a short story and it's not a long novel. Also, the story moves from London to the countryside, so it replicates one of my favorite tropes in comic literature: city people going into the country where they learn something of value they can bring back to their city lives. It's the prototypical pattern of *As You Like It* and *The Beaux' Strategem* and dozens of other plays and novels. I think there's a sturdiness to that shift in geography.

Do you consider yourself primarily a writer of comedies? Why do you think you tend toward that form?

I think the answer is simply that I write what I love and what I care about. The great Shakespeare comedies that inspire us all – *Twelfth Night, Much Ado…, Midsummer,* and the rest – are works of divine intervention and beyond imitation. But what I can aspire to – in the same way a cat can look at a king – are plays like *The Rivals* and *The School for Scandal, She Stoops to Conquer* and *Private Lives* and *The Importance of Being Earnest.* These are the works of literature that I just love in my bones. They are bound up with the nature of good fellowship and humanity, and nothing else delights me or interests me in the way that they do. So what I've done is spent my life trying to write them.

For J.W. Morrissette
who knows so much about the theatre it should be illegal,
and in gratitude for many years of friendship and good cheer.

ACT ONE

(In the darkness, music begins. Something troubling from the Romantic repertoire. Perhaps the opening of the First Movement of Mahler's Symphony No. 3 in D Major. It suggests the murky atmosphere of the moors of England, the gloomy, dangerous world of fog and quicksand, criminals and beasts.)

Prologue: The Yew Alley at Baskerville Hall, late 1890s

(Baskerville Hall is on the Moors of Devonshire, and the night is filled with the sucking, breathing sounds of danger. Out of the mist appears SIR CHARLES BASKERVILLE, a middle-aged man in faultless attire. He steps out of his back door –)

SIR CHARLES. I'll be back in a moment, Barrymore. Just enjoying the garden.

BARRYMORE. *(off)* Very good, Sir Charles.

(– and walks down the grass alley between the famous Baskerville yew trees. He stops at the gate and looks around as though he is expecting someone. But no one is there. He checks his pocket watch. Perhaps he's early. He lights a cigar. He takes a puff … at which moment he hears something strange. Then we hear it. It's the sound of something terrible and large, breathing heavily in the distance. He looks up, slightly alarmed. He looks in one direction, then another. The breathing gets louder. Then he sees it. Something is approaching.)

SIR CHARLES. No … no … Stay back. Stay where you are …

(SIR CHARLES backs away. We hear the sound of something approaching SIR CHARLES, first at a walk, then at a gallop. SIR CHARLES turns and runs, screaming.)

SIR CHARLES. *Get away! Stay there! Stay away from me!*

(The music builds. A shadow looms up and springs at SIR CHARLES and we hear the roar of something almost supernatural.)

SOUND. *ROOOOOOOAAAAAAARRRRR!*

SIR CHARLES. *AHHHHHHHHHH!*

(The lights black out before we can see what has happened to SIR CHARLES.)

Scene One: 221B Baker Street, the Residence of Mr. Sherlock Holmes

(The lights come up to reveal DOCTOR WATSON standing in the sitting room. WATSON is solid and reliable, the Sancho Panza to Holmes's Don Quixote. Nearby is DAISY, the scullery maid, in a mob cap, scrubbing the floor. There is a window to the street and we hear the sound of carriages on the cobblestones below.)

WATSON. *(to the audience)* It all began, as these things do, with simplicity itself: a walking stick, left at our residence by an unknown visitor. However, the trail, like a labyrinth out of an ancient myth, led eventually to what my friend Sherlock Holmes described as the greatest and most dangerous case in the history of his career. It ended with a kind of reckless triumph, and along the way it renewed my respect for the greatest man I have ever known.

(MRS. HUDSON enters with the stick. She's the housekeeper and is full of warmth and good spirit.)

MRS. HUDSON. Oh Doctor Watson, look at this cane. That man last night left it here by accident when you and Mr. Holmes were out at the opera. Oh it's so romantic leaving a stick like this by the fireside.

(**SHERLOCK HOLMES** *enters. He is lean and moody, a bundle of energy and intelligence. He is in a good mood.*)

HOLMES. Good morning, Watson.

WATSON. 'Morning, Holmes.

DAISY. 'Morning.

MRS. HUDSON. Have you seen the cane yet, Mr. Holmes? I wonder who left it?

HOLMES. *(examining the cane)* Hmm, well, that's not a problem now is it? The inscription says right here on the ferrule: "To Doctor John Mortimer: good luck from his friends at the CCH, 1894." What do you make of it, Watson?

(He hands the cane to his friend.)

WATSON. Well applying your methods, Holmes, though I'm sure I can never equal them, I'd say that because the stick is scratched on the bottom, the man likes to take long walks and he lives in the country. Therefore, CCH stands for "Country Club Hunt." And because such a gift is generally given upon retirement, I'd say that the fellow's a successful, elderly medical man who has lived in the country his entire life and is obviously well-beloved by his friends.

HOLMES. Excellent, Watson. Truly remarkable.

WATSON. Am I correct then?

HOLMES. No, you're completely wrong.

WATSON. Really, Holmes –

HOLMES. But you inspire me, Watson. Like John Falstaff, you are not only witty in yourself, but the cause that wit is in other men. In point of fact, as the cane tells us, our Doctor Mortimer is a young man under thirty who used to work at Charing Cross Hospital – "CCH" – here in London. He has lived in the country for the past five years, and he is amiable, unambitious, absent-minded, and the possessor of a favorite medium-sized dog.

MRS. HUDSON. Oh Mr. Holmes, sometimes I think I'd marry you if you didn't have such filthy habits.

HOLMES. Trifles, Mrs. Hudson. A parlor game. He is *Doctor* Mortimer, so "CCH" must stand for Charing Cross Hospital, and he must be a *young* man because he wouldn't leave such a fine practice if he were well established. So he must have been a student there, and as the date on the stick is five years old, we have a young fellow, under thirty.

WATSON. And the rest of it?

HOLMES. The scratches on the cane confirm that he does indeed live in the country now, and it is my experience that only *amiable* men receive testimonials, only *unambitious* ones abandon London, and only *absent-minded* ones leave their sticks and not their visiting-cards.

DAISY. Gor.

MRS. HUDSON. And what about the dog?

HOLMES. Look at the tooth marks.

(He holds the stick to his mouth sideways and demonstrates.)

Being a heavy stick, the dog has held it tightly by the middle. The dog's jaw, as shown in the space between the marks, is too broad for a terrier and too narrow for a mastiff. It may have been, aha, yes it is! It's a curly-haired spaniel.

WATSON. Holmes, please! How could you possibly know that?

HOLMES. Because I'm looking out the window and see the dog on our doorstep now,

(Ring!)

and there is the ring of its owner. Mrs. Hudson, the door?

MRS. HUDSON. Right away, sir.

(*She goes off.*)

HOLMES. Now is the dramatic moment of fate, Watson, when you hear a step upon the stair of someone walking into your life, and you know not whether for good or ill. What does Dr. Mortimer, man of science, ask of Sherlock Holmes, specialist in crime? And can he relieve the tedium of our mortal existence? Come in!

(**DR. MORTIMER** *enters with* **MRS. HUDSON**. *He's about thirty, sparkling, friendly eyes, gold-rimmed glasses.*)

DR. MORTIMER. Ah, my stick! What a relief. I wouldn't lose it for the world.

HOLMES. A presentation, I see.

DR. MORTIMER. Indeed. From Charing Cross Hospital when I moved to the country. I was a student at the time.

(**HOLMES** *gives* **WATSON** *a look.*)

I take it I am addressing Mr. Sherlock Holmes.

HOLMES. And this is my friend, Doctor Watson.

WATSON. How do you do.

MRS. HUDSON. Ahem.

HOLMES. And this is Mrs. Hudson.

MRS. HUDSON. How do you do, sir.

HOLMES. Tea, Mrs. Hudson?

MRS. HUDSON. Yes, I'd love some. Hm? Oh of course. Right away.

(*She exits.*)

DR. MORTIMER. Shall I begin, sir?

HOLMES. Please.

DR. MORTIMER. I have here a manuscript –

HOLMES. Mid-eighteenth century, unless it's a forgery.

DR. MORTIMER. 1742 to be exact. Handed down for over a century and committed to me for safe-keeping

by my friend Sir Charles Baskerville, whose sudden
death three weeks ago created so much excitement in
Devonshire.

WATSON. It appears to be a statement of some sort.

DR. MORTIMER. May I read it to you?

*(**HOLMES** nods and settles down to listen.)*

HOLMES. Have a seat.

DR. MORTIMER. "Of the origins of the Hound of the
Baskervilles:"

(Eerie, troubling music begins to play in the background.)

WATSON. "Hound?"

DR. MORTIMER. "Know then, that in the time of the Great
Rebellion, the Manor of Baskerville was held by one
Hugo, of a most wild, profane and godless nature."

*(Thunder. The story that **DR. MORTIMER** is recounting
begins to unfold in front of us, and **DAISY** turns into
SIR HUGO BASKERVILLE before our eyes.)*

"It chanced that this Hugo came to love the daughter
of a yeoman who held lands near Baskerville, but the
maiden feared his evil ways and would ever avoid him."

"So it came to pass that one Michaelmas this Hugo,
with five or six of his wicked companions, stole down
upon the farm of the maiden and carried her off. And
when they brought her to Baskerville Hall, the maiden
was placed in an upper chamber – "

MAIDEN. *No, stop it, please!*

HUGO. *(striking her) Quiet down!*

MAIDEN. *Ah!*

DR. MORTIMER. "– while Hugo and his friends sat down to
a long carouse, as was their custom."

(Singing and carousing is heard.)

"Now the poor lass upstairs was like to have her wits
turned by the singing and shouting, and in the stress
of fear, she did that which might have daunted the
bravest of men, for by the aid of the ivy which covered

the south wall, she came down from the eaves and so began homeward across the moor. Now it chanced that some small time later, Hugo found the cage empty and the bird escaped, whereupon, rushing down the stairs he sprang upon the table and cried:"

HUGO. *If I can but overtake that wench this very night, I shall render up my body to the Powers of Evil!*

(crash of thunder)

Now saddle my mare, unkennel my pack AND PUT THE HOUNDS UPON HER!!

(We hear thundering hooves and the hounds baying in their bloodlust.)

DR. MORTIMER. "Taking to their horses in pursuit, the revelers had gone but a mile when they passed a shepherdess and cried to her to know if she had seen the hunt. The woman was crazed with fear and could scarcely speak, but at last recounted:"

SHEPHERDESS. I have seen the maiden and the dogs, and then Sir Hugo passed me upon his mare and there ran behind him *such a hound of Hell as man has never looked upon!*

DR. MORTIMER. "The drunken squires rode on, but soon their skins turned cold for they came upon the dogs who, though known for the valor of their breed, were whimpering in a cluster at the head of a ditch;"

(sounds of the dogs whimpering)

"and there in the moonlight lay the unhappy maiden where she had fallen dead of fear. But it was not the sight of her body nor that of Sir Hugo lying nearby which raised the hair upon their heads, but standing over him and plucking at his throat was a foul thing, a great black beast shaped like a hound yet larger than any hound that ever mortal eye has rested upon."

(We hear the hideous, snarling, tearing sounds of a horrid beast.)

"And even as they looked, the thing tore the throat out of Sir Hugo."

HUGO. *Arghhhhh!*

(As **HUGO** *and the* **MAIDEN** *disappear,* **DR. MORTIMER** *closes the manuscript. There is a dead, almost eerie silence.)*

HOLMES. … Continue.

DR. MORTIMER. I am here because of the sudden death three weeks ago of my friend and patient Sir Charles Baskerville at the very same estate in Devon. The verdict at the inquest was death by natural causes.

WATSON. But?

DR. MORTIMER. But I got there before the police came, and at the inquest I was reluctant to reveal certain … observations I made at the time for fear of endorsing local superstitions.

HOLMES. I'm fond of "observations," Doctor. Pray continue.

DR. MORTIMER. The day had been wet and the footprints of Sir Charles reveal him walking behind the house to the gate, where he seems to have waited. He then continued, but his footprints changed – he appears to have walked on *tiptoe* from that point on, moving *away* from the house to the spot where he fell. I then examined the body, which had not been touched.

(Eerie music begins; **SIR CHARLES** *is lying on the ground.)*

Sir Charles lay face down, his arms out, his fingers dug into the ground, and when I turned him over, his features were convulsed with such strong emotion that I could hardly have sworn to his identity. There was certainly no physical injury of any kind, and while there was no disturbance *near* the body, there were marks on the ground several yards away.

WATSON. Footprints?

DR. MORTIMER. Footprints.

HOLMES. A man or a woman's?

DR. MORTIMER. Mr. Holmes, they were the footprints of a gigantic hound.

(A screech of sound. The dialogue becomes rapid-fire.)

HOLMES. You saw this?

DR. MORTIMER. Clearly.

HOLMES. And you said nothing?

DR. MORTIMER. What was the use?

HOLMES. How was it that no one else saw it?

DR. MORTIMER. The marks were twenty yards from the body.

WATSON. There are sheep dogs on the moor?

DR. MORTIMER. This was no sheep dog.

HOLMES. You say it was large?

DR. MORTIMER. Enormous.

HOLMES. *Oh, if I had only been there! You should have sent for me!*

DR. MORTIMER. I didn't think of it. Besides …

WATSON. What is it? You hesitate.

DR. MORTIMER. There were incidents before the tragedy. Several people saw a creature upon the moor which corresponds exactly with the Baskerville demon of legend, a creature from a nightmare, with blazing eyes and dripping jaws. *Gentlemen, there is such a reign of terror in the district that no one will even cross the moor at night!*

HOLMES. *(quietly)* How can we assist you?

DR. MORTIMER. By advising me what I should do with Sir *Henry* Baskerville, who arrives at Waterloo Station in exactly one hour.

WATSON. He is the heir?

DR. MORTIMER. Yes. He's an American who lives in Texas.

WATSON. Why not take him to the home of his fathers?

DR. MORTIMER. But consider the history. The danger! What can I *do*, gentlemen?!

HOLMES. First I advise you to call off your spaniel, who is scratching at my front door with the zeal of a Christian, then take a cab and collect Sir Henry.

DR. MORTIMER. And then?

HOLMES. Then return here tomorrow morning at ten with Sir Henry and I will suggest how to proceed. Good morning.

WATSON. Goodbye.

DR. MORTIMER. Goodbye.

(**DR. MORTIMER** *leaves the room.*)

HOLMES. I like it, Watson. There is a feverish quality to this unlikely tale that appeals to me. Are you going out?

WATSON. Unless I can help you in some way.

HOLMES. No, dear fellow, but when you pass Bradley's, would you ask them to send up a pound of their strongest shag tobacco.

WATSON. (*to the audience*) This was the moment when everything changed. Holmes had smelled the bait, and I sensed that we were on the verge of another one of his strange, roller-coaster adventures. I also knew that tobacco was the engine he required at these moments of intense, mental concentration, so I stopped at Bradley's.

BRADLEY. That'll be two and sixpence for the best shag tobacco in the country.

(*He smells it.*)

Ahhhh.

WATSON. I had it sent 'round, then returned that evening.

Scene Two: That Evening

(**WATSON** *enters the room and is overwhelmed by a dense cloud of tobacco smoke. He chokes and waves his arms and gasps, as* **HOLMES** *appears in the middle of it, puffing away on his pipe.*)

WATSON. *(choking)* Holmes … Holmes …

HOLMES. Caught cold, dear man?

WATSON. No, it's this poisonous atmosphere!

HOLMES. It is rather thick, but as a medical man you will admit that smoking is good for the health.

(**DAISY** *emits her distinctive laugh.*)

WATSON. You know I admit no such thing. Now, how is the case coming?

HOLMES. *(casually changing his tie at a mirror)* There are certainly some points of distinction about it. That change in the footprints, for example. What do you make of that?

WATSON. Mortimer said the victim began walking on tip-toe at some point.

HOLMES. He was running, Watson, running desperately for his life until his heart burst and he fell dead on the spot.

WATSON. Running from what?

HOLMES. There lies our problem. There are indications that the man was literally crazed with fear.

WATSON. His face you mean?

HOLMES. That and I believe that something dangerous approached him from across the moor. Only a man who has lost his wits would run *from* the house instead of towards it when he was threatened. But who was he waiting for that night? And why was he waiting in the Yew Alley instead of inside the house? The thing takes shape, Watson. It becomes coherent. Come, get your hat, we'll be late.

WATSON. For what?

HOLMES. For the opera! There is nothing like a little musical mayhem to clear the mind.

Scene Three: A Box at the Royal Opera House, Covent Garden

(**HOLMES** *is seated, in his own world, as* **WATSON** *addresses us. From the stage below we hear the end of Act Two of* Tosca *as* **BARON SCARPIA** *brutalizes* **FLORIA TOSCA** *and she takes her revenge by stabbing him to death.*)

WATSON. As always at the opera, Holmes sat there motionless, as though in a trance induced by the discordant harmonies that swirled around us.

(*We hear the divine music echoing through the theater and we see* **TOSCA** *stabbing* **SCARPIA** *on the stage below the box.*)

I have no doubt, however, that his brain was racing a mile a minute, sorting clues like a ciphering machine, while on the stage below us a woman named Floria Tosca was taking her revenge on the evil Baron Scarpia, acting out the kind of ruthless murder that had become part of our daily lives.

(*Bing bong! A doorbell rings and we're back at:*)

Scene Four: 221B Baker Street, the Next Morning

MRS. HUDSON. Doctor John Mortimer and Sir Henry Baskerville, Baronet. *Entrez s'il vous plaît.*

(**MRS. HUDSON** *exits.* **SIR HENRY** *is a handsome young man, full of charm and innocence. He has a Texas accent, not a silly one, but pronounced.*)

SIR HENRY. Gentlemen, it's good to meet ya.

WATSON. Likewise. It's a pleasure.

SIR HENRY. I understand, Mr. Holmes, that you think out little puzzles for people, and if mah new friend here hadn't arranged for us to come 'round this mornin', I'd have come myself.

HOLMES. You have had a remarkable experience, then?

SIR HENRY. I wouldn't call it remarkable, exactly. Just this oddball letter that arrived at my hotel this mornin'.

HOLMES. *(reading the address on the envelope)* "To Sir Henry Baskerville, Northumberland Hotel." Who knew you were going to the Northumberland?

DR. MORTIMER. No one could have possibly known.

HOLMES. Except yourself.

DR. MORTIMER. Well, yes, but we only decided to stay there after we met at the station.

*(**HOLMES** removes the letter from the envelope and unfolds it – and behind the **ACTORS** we see it projected or otherwise displayed. [See Appendix.] It consists of several words cut out of a newspaper and glued to a piece of paper – all except the last word, which is written in ink.)*

WATSON. Good heavens! All the words have been cut out of a magazine or a newspaper.

HOLMES. Except the last one. "As you value your life or your reason, keep away from the moor."

(examining the letter minutely, holding it an inch from his nose and smelling it)

I take it you've told Sir Henry about the hound.

DR. MORTIMER. Yes I have –

SIR HENRY. And it sounds like hogwash to me. A big ol' hound with blazin' eyes who breathes fire? Hell, I got hounds back home that would eat him for breakfast and spit out the bones.

HOLMES. Watson, do we have yesterday's *Times?*

WATSON. Right here.

HOLMES. There's an interesting article on the front page about Free Trade. Listen carefully. "You will see that it stands to reason that your tariffs will keep away wealth from the life of the country, which … "

SIR HENRY. Aren't you gettin' a bit off the trail here?

HOLMES. On the contrary, I am hot *on* the trail. See the words in this article: "you," "your," "life," "reason," "keep away," "from the." You see the words in this letter – "you," "your," "life," "reason," "keep away," "from the" – they were cut out of a copy of this very article.

DR. MORTIMER. That's remarkable! How did you know that?

HOLMES. Come now, Doctor. It is my profession. I know the print of every newspaper in the country – though I will confess that once, when I was very young, I confused the *Dover Express* with the *Oxford Mercury*. I couldn't leave my house for weeks.

SIR HENRY. But why is the word "moor" written out by hand?

WATSON. The word is less common and therefore harder to find in print.

HOLMES. Well done, Watson.

WATSON. Thank you, Holmes.

HOLMES. Now tell me, gentlemen, have you observed anyone following you this morning?

SIR HENRY. Holy cow, it's like I've walked straight into a dime novel.

DR. MORTIMER. I've seen no one.

WATSON. The point remains whether Sir Henry should go to Devonshire or not.

SIR HENRY. No it don't remain! That is my property now – all ten thousand acres of it – and I ain't givin' it up for nobody.

HOLMES. Then do as I say and do it now. I want the two of you to *walk back* to your hotel at a brisk but not unreasonable pace. Doctor Watson and I will then join you there for lunch at one. Good morning, gentlemen. Go quickly.

SIR HENRY. I gotta confess, I don't quite understand why we're –

HOLMES. *Do not question me! Go now!*

WATSON. We shall see you later.

(*The two men hurry out. The moment they're gone,* **HOLMES** *springs into action.*)

HOLMES. Quick, Watson! Your hat! Not a moment to lose!

WATSON. What? What's the matter?! Shall I stop them?!

HOLMES. Not for the world, dear friend. We'll follow them at about fifty yards! Quickly, quickly! Into the street!

Scene Five: Through the London Streets

(*It's pouring rain and we hear the sound of it. We also hear a boom of thunder. We follow* **HOLMES** *and* **WATSON** *out the door and through the streets of London as they keep* **SIR HENRY** *and* **DR. MORTIMER** *in view. The street is crowded and full of street noises.*)

WATSON. Good Lord, it's pouring out here!

HOLMES. Keep them in view!

WATSON. There they are!

HOLMES. Stay low. Act natural.

(*They pull their hats down.*)

WATSON. Holmes! Look! They're stopping at a window!

HOLMES. Duck in this doorway! Look, there! Do you see that cab with the man inside? The one with the black beard?

(*We see him.*)

It's halted on the other side of the street ... and now it's moving slowly forward again ... it's following Sir Henry and Doctor Mortimer ...

(*Suddenly the* **MAN** *turns and stares directly at* **HOLMES** *and* **WATSON.**)

WATSON. Oh, I say! He's spotted us!

MAN WITH BLACK BEARD. Sherlock Holmes!

HOLMES. Get back!

WATSON. Too late!

MAN WITH BLACK BEARD. *(screaming to his driver) Move! Move at a gallop!*

(We hear the whinny of a horse and the carriage hurrying away over the cobblestones.)

WATSON. *There he goes!*

MAN WITH BLACK BEARD. *Quickly! Quickly!*

HOLMES. *Watson, find us a cab immediately!*

(He and WATSON *try to hail one.)*

WATSON. Taxi! Taxi!

HOLMES. *Cab! Cab! Where's a cab, for God's sake! … Ah! How could I be such a dolt! An idiot! My God, I'm a babe in the woods!* I trust, Watson, if you're an honest man, you will record this blunder of mine in your memoirs along with the successes you keep writing about!

WATSON. Who was the man?

HOLMES. I have no idea.

WATSON. But how did you know that he'd – ?

HOLMES. Watson, please. It was evident from all we heard that Sir Henry has been closely shadowed since arriving in London. But I thought his pursuer would be on foot, not in a cab.

WATSON. It's a pity we didn't get the number.

HOLMES. *(a look)* My dear Watson. As clumsy as I've been, you don't think I failed to get the number, do you? I have an idea, come with me. Yes, there it is, the Messenger Office. Come inside!

(HOLMES *leads the way into:)*

Scene Six: A District Messenger Office

(We hear the jingle of a bell as they enter. An exuberant man named WILSON *is behind the counter.)*

WILSON. Mr. Holmes! Oh my goodness! What a pleasure to see you so *LUCY! IT'S MR. HOLMES AND DOCTOR WATSON!* I'm afraid she's going a bit deaf like her mother, who couldn't hear a freight train if it was runnin' her down but *LUCY!*

(**LUCY** *runs in.*)

LUCY. Oh my saints, it's Mr. Holmes and the dear Doctor! Oh, we'll never forget what you gentlemen did for us.

WILSON. We'd have no business left!

LUCY. He'd be rotting in jail as he ought to be.

WILSON. Owwww.

WATSON. You're lovely to say it.

LUCY. What?

WATSON. *YOU'RE LOVELY!*

LUCY. Ooh, Doctor! *(flirting)* Last man who called me lovely is the father of me children.

WILSON. Now what can I do for you gentlemen?

HOLMES. Just two items. First, I'd like to send a wire to the Cab Authority. Tell them I seek the identity of the woman who drives Cab Number 2704. *[spoken as "twenty-seven-oh-four"]*

WATSON. "Woman?"

HOLMES. Come, Watson, you didn't notice?

WILSON. I'll do it this instant, sir.

HOLMES. Also, amongst your messenger boys I recall you have a lad named Cartwright who has done some errands for me in the past. Is he here?

LUCY. Who?

WATSON. *CARTWRIGHT!*

LUCY. Oh he's a good lad, he is. I'll call him for you. He's been one of our regulars since *CARTWRIGHT, GET DOWN HERE! IT'S MR. HOLMES TO SEE YOU!*

CARTWRIGHT. *(off)* Coming, ma'am!

HOLMES. And if you would be so kind, I'd like a moment alone with him.

LUCY. What?

WILSON. *Be quiet!*

WATSON. *ALONE!*

LUCY. *(taking his hand)* Of course you feel alone, Doctor, you need a wife to take care of you.

WILSON. *CARTWRIGHT!!*

CARTWRIGHT. *(entering)* I'm right 'ere, sir.

(**CARTWRIGHT** *is a boy of fourteen, a street urchin with a Cockney accent. He wears a cap and has a ready smile.*)

WILSON. We'll leave you to it.

LUCY. What? What?

WILSON. *WE'RE GOING AWAY!*

LUCY. No, I don't think we should stay …

(They're gone.)

[shake hands aggressively with both]

CARTWRIGHT. 'Allo, Mr. 'Olmes. Doctor.

HOLMES. Hello, Cartwright. How are the rest of the boys?

CARTWRIGHT. The Irregulars, sir? They're doin' all right with the odd job now and then. O' course they wouldn't mind a little extra work on their plates if it came a-callin' in the scheme o' things.

(A boy named **MILKER** *pops in. Another street urchin.)*

MILKER. We certainly wouldn't!

WATSON. Who's that?

MILKER. The name's Milker, sir. I work with Cartwright when there's a shilling or two in circulation, if ya see what I mean. So what d'ya think?

HOLMES. Fine, fine, it will speed things up. Now do you boys see this Hotel Directory?

(**HOLMES** *has taken it from one of Wilson's shelves.*)

There are twenty-three hotels listed in the neighborhood of Charing Cross.

CARTWRIGHT. I see 'em.

Start to leave

MILKER. Got it.

HOLMES. You will visit each of them in turn.

CARTWRIGHT. Yes, sir *(Start to leave)*

HOLMES. *(giving them money)* You will begin in each case by giving the porter one shilling.

MILKER. Yes, sir. *(Start to leave)*

HOLMES. You will tell him that you want to see yesterday's refuse. You will say that you're looking for a lost telegram.

CARTWRIGHT. Yes, sir. *(Start to leave)*

HOLMES. But what you are really looking for is this page of *The Times* with some words cut out.

MILKER. Yes, sir. *(Start to leave)*

HOLMES. Will you both stop saying "Yes, sir?"

CARTWRIGHT & MILKER. Yes, sir. *(stay)*

HOLMES. Now in about twenty cases the waste of the day before will have been burned, but in the three other cases you will be shown a heap of paper and you will look for this page of *The Times* among it. The odds are enormously against your finding it, and I'd like a report as soon as possible.

MILKER. Yes, s –

CARTWRIGHT. You got it, sir.

MILKER. And may I say what a pleasure it is entering your employment, Mr. Holmes –

CARTWRIGHT. and you Doctor Watson

MILKER. and now *(As he is talking, go Downstage right, right of Milker)*

CARTWRIGHT. like a runaway 'orse

MILKER. or a speeding train

CARTWRIGHT. or a spotted leopard

MILKER. or a genie in a bottle

CARTWRIGHT. or a phantom

MILKER. or a ghost

CARTWRIGHT. or a bullet

MILKER. or a sound

CARTWRIGHT & MILKER. *we're off!*

(*They run off.*)

HOLMES. Watson, come. We are due at the Northumberland Hotel and I know the desk clerk there. He's a Castilian.

Scene Seven: The Lobby of the Northumberland Hotel

(*Behind the counter is a **CASTILIAN DESK CLERK** with an unctuous manner and pronounced accent.*)

DESK CLERK. *Meethter Holmes!* What a pleasure, thir. And *Doctor Watthon!* Oh I read about your exthploits in the Thtrand Magazine *religiouthly.* Thir Henry Baskerville is exthpecting you upsthairs, thir.

HOLMES. Have you any objection to my looking at your register?

DESK CLERK. Oh, not in the leatht, thir. Mi regithterio eth tu regithterio.

HOLMES. Ah, I see that no one has checked in since Sir Henry arrived.

DESK CLERK. That ith correct, thir. We try to keep out the rift and the raft becauth, ath you know, our hotel ith the most proper in all of London.

(*During the following, the **DESK CLERK** tries to listen to what **HOLMES** is telling **WATSON**, but tries to cover it by playing with the plant on his desk or some such.*)

HOLMES. (*aside to **WATSON***) This is very interesting. If no one's checked in, it means that the man in the cab is anxious to *watch* Sir Henry but equally anxious not to be *seen* by him.

WATSON. You mean he might be recognized – ? Well look who's coming.

(**INSPECTOR LESTRADE** *enters. He's a blustery, unrepentant member of Scotland Yard with a loud voice*

that has the timbre of a meat grinder. He's overflowing
with self-confidence and a lack of irony. He speaks with
a lower-middle-class accent.)

HOLMES. It's an old friend.

WATSON. Inspector Lestrade of Scotland Yard.

HOLMES. Let's hope he does not derail the investigation
this time.

LESTRADE. Well, knock me senseless, it's Mr. Sherlock
'Olmes. What the 'ell are you doin' here? 'Ello, Doctor.

HOLMES. I'm meeting a client. What about you?

LESTRADE. They're wastin' me bleedin' time with some
piss-pot baloney about some baronet.

DESK CLERK. Thir, your language, pleath!

LESTRADE. What about it?

DESK CLERK. Thith ith a public hothtilery and we have
children here!

(*A baby carriage rolls across stage.*)

BABY. (*inside the carriage*) WHHHHAAAAAAAAAAA!

DESK CLERK. Do you thee what you've done?! *Ay Dios mio*
en España! Hasta cuanto tengo que soportar a este insolente
insultando y desgraciando la honra de mi hotel?!

LESTRADE. I ain't impressed! Me mother speaks Italian,
too.

(*to* HOLMES)

If you ask me it's a lot o' bollocks for some toff from
America who's goin' to inherit a fortune anyhow.

HOLMES. He's my client, actually.

LESTRADE. Good, 'cause I got a more important case in
'Ounslow involvin'

(*directed at the* DESK CLERK *to defy him*)

some bleedin' bastard and his naked mistresses!

DESK CLERK. *Ayeeee!*

(LESTRADE *exits.*)

BABY. *WHHHHAAAAAAAAA!*

DESK CLERK. *Theeth ith outrageous! He ith thpoiling the prethtige of theeth hotel and he will ruin uth!!!*

(**SIR HENRY** *enters holding a black boot.*)

SIR HENRY. Galdarnit!

HOLMES. Sir Henry. What's the matter?

SIR HENRY. I'll tell ya what the matter is! They're playin' me for a sucker in this hotel! And if they don't find my boot, there's gonna be trouble!

WATSON. You lost a boot?

SIR HENRY. Not just a boot – it's my favorite pair! And they lost just *one of 'em!* Now does that make any sense in the world?! *Hey you!*

(*A* **GERMAN MAID** *has entered, crossing the lobby. Perhaps the* **DESK CLERK** *has summoned her and then gone off.*)

GERMAN MAID. *Mein Gott!*

SIR HENRY. She's the maid. I talked to her earlier. Miss, have you found my boot yet?! Now tell me the truth, 'cause if you were in on it – !

GERMAN MAID. Nein, nein, sir! I have not found der boot, I svear. I'm asken der boot-black und iss not mitt him. Und I look in der cupboard und I look on der shelves und I make der qveries –

SIR HENRY. Well either that boot comes back before sundown or I'll talk to your manager!

GERMAN MAID. I find, I promise! I find das boot!

(**DR. MORTIMER** *enters in a warm coat from the street.*)

HOLMES. Ah, Doctor Mortimer –

DR. MORTIMER. I'm sorry I'm late. Brr, it's cold!

GERMAN MAID. *(asking to take the Doctor's hat)* Bitte.

DR. MORTIMER. It's more than bitter, it's downright freezing.

GERMAN MAID. Danke.

DR. MORTIMER. Yes it's dank as well.

(He shivers, and the **MAID** *exits with his hat.)*

SIR HENRY. I'm sorry, Mr. Holmes. It just gets in my craw when somebody tries to play me for a sucker. I know it ain't important in the scheme o' things ...

HOLMES. On the contrary, I believe it's quite important.

WATSON. You do realize that you were followed this morning after you left us.

DR. MORTIMER. Really?

SIR HENRY. By who?!

HOLMES. Dr. Mortimer, do any of your acquaintances in Devonshire have a black beard?

DR. MORTIMER. Barrymore does. Sir Charles's butler.

WATSON. And did Barrymore profit by Sir Charles's will?

DR. MORTIMER. He and his wife were left five hundred pounds each. But I trust a bequest doesn't make one a suspect. I received ... well, ten thousand pounds.

WATSON. That's a lot of money.

DR. MORTIMER. Yes, it is.

HOLMES. Anyone else?

DR. MORTIMER. He left a bit to a few charities, and the residue went to Sir Henry.

HOLMES. And how much was that?

DR. MORTIMER. Seven hundred and forty thousand pounds.

WATSON. *Good God!* Excuse me.

HOLMES. Quite enough money to provoke a murder, don't you think?

SIR HENRY. When Dr. Mortimer told me the amount of the legacy I almost fell off mah chair.

HOLMES. And if anything happened to Sir Henry, who would inherit?

DR. MORTIMER. Well I've heard talk of a black-sheep son of Sir Charles's brother Roger, but I believe he died some years ago in South America.

HOLMES. *(to* **SIR HENRY***)* And you're unmarried?

SIR HENRY. That's right.

HOLMES. No children?

SIR HENRY. I sure hope not, but I can't swear to it. Ha!

WATSON. Have you made a will?

SIR HENRY. Nope.

HOLMES. Hmm. Well. I agree that you should go to Devonshire and claim your inheritance. There is only one proviso: you must not go alone.

SIR HENRY. Dr. Mortimer's goin' with me.

HOLMES. But Dr. Mortimer has his practice to attend to, and I presume that his house is not near the Manor.

DR. MORTIMER. Four miles away.

HOLMES. There you are. You must take someone trustworthy who will stay by your side.

SIR HENRY. Could you come yourself?

HOLMES. I'm afraid that's impossible. There is a scandal threatening the King of Bohemia that requires my attention at the moment. However, if my friend would agree, you could have no better companion, nor any braver.

WATSON. Me? Oh, I say, that's a kind way to put it.

SIR HENRY. And it would be kind of you, Doctor, if you're up for it.

WATSON. Well. Hm. I'm not really sure I'm the man for it, but … I'll do it.

HOLMES. Excellent!

SIR HENRY. Okay!

DR. MORTIMER. The matter's concluded then. When shall we depart?

HOLMES. Shall we say Paddington Station today at four?

SIR HENRY. Done.

ALL. Done!

("Owheeeeeeeee!" The train.)

Scene Eight: The Platform at Paddington Station

(We hear the scream of a train whistle, then the noises of a bustling train station. A blast of smoke fills the air, and **HOLMES** *and* **WATSON** *confer on the platform.)*

HOLMES. Watson, you'll write to me frequently and report the facts. You are my eyes and ears and I must know everything. Now I've made some inquiries and learned that a man escaped last month from Princetown Prison, which is close to Baskerville, and he's said to be dangerous. There is also a scientist named Stapleton living nearby with his sister, as well as the butler and his wife, the Barrymores, of whom I hear rather sinister rumors, and of course our friend, Dr. Mortimer, who I believe to be honest but of whom we actually know very little.

WATSON. You should be more trusting, Holmes.

HOLMES. Oh I'd be much more trusting if he hadn't inherited ten thousand pounds. On which theory we should add Sir Henry himself to our little gallery.

WATSON. Oh I don't believe that. He's so American.

HOLMES. Well he inherited close to a million pounds, and *someone* killed Sir Charles Baskerville.

*(***MRS. CLAYTON***, a cab woman, approaches. She's as tough as shoe leather and about as attractive.)*

MRS. CLAYTON. Oy there! 'Scuse me. Are you the owners o' the 'ouse at 221B Baker Street?

WATSON. That's right.

MRS. CLAYTON. I understand you wanted some words with the driver of Cab Number 2704, now what d'you got against me?

HOLMES. I have nothing against you, Madam. On the contrary, I have half a sovereign for you if you'll answer some questions.

MRS. CLAYTON. Well I'm havin' a good day, aren't I? How can I 'elp ya?

HOLMES. Tell me about the man with the black beard who watched my house at ten this morning, then followed two gentlemen down Regent Street.

MRS. CLAYTON. Now what's the good o' me tellin' you? You know as much I do already! The gent told me 'e was a detective and that I was to keep me trap shut, as it were.

WATSON. My good woman, this is serious business, and you'll find yourself in a bad position if you try to hide anything!

HOLMES. Tell me where you picked him up and all that occurred.

MRS. CLAYTON. Well, this gentleman 'ailed me at 'alf past noyne this mornin' at Trafalgar Square and offered me two guineas if I would do as 'e wanted. First we drove to the Northumberland and waited there till two gents come out, and we followed 'em till they stopped at your place.

HOLMES. And then?

MRS. CLAYTON. They come out o' there and we followed 'em again, only this time my gentleman sees you on the street and 'e throws up the trap and cries "*Oy! You! Drive as 'ard as you can to Waterloo Station!*" and I got 'im there in ten minutes and away 'e went.

HOLMES. And who was this detective of yours? Did he give a name?

MRS. CLAYTON. Yes 'e did. As 'e left the cab, 'e said, "It might interest you to know, young woman, that you 'ave been drivin' Mr. Sherlock 'Olmes."

HOLMES. What?

WATSON. What?!

*(And **HOLMES** breaks into a peal of laughter.)*

HOLMES. Thank you, good woman. You have been very helpful.

MRS. CLAYTON. Thank *you*, sir.

*(**MRS. CLAYTON** exits.)*

HOLMES. What a foe, Watson! The cunning rascal! He spotted who I was in Regent Street, assumed I would find the driver of the cab, and sent me back this audacious message. I tell you, Watson, this time we have a foeman worthy of our steel.

WATSON. The man is bold, if nothing else.

HOLMES. He's a creature of tangles who is weaving a web whose intricacies we are barely glimpsing. I'm afraid I'm not easy about sending you on this dangerous errand. You have a revolver, I suppose?

WATSON. *(pats his coat pocket)* Yes, I thought it well to take it with me.

HOLMES. Keep it near you night and day and never relax your precautions. Ah, Doctor Mortimer, Sir Henry. Right on time.

(**DR. MORTIMER** *and* **SIR HENRY** *enter and the train whistles.*)

SIR HENRY. Well if this ain't an adventure, I don't know what is.

WATSON. Did you find your boot?

DR. MORTIMER. He did not. I suppose it's gone forever.

HOLMES. How very intriguing. Sir Henry, heed what I say and follow my instructions to the letter.

SIR HENRY. Instructions?

HOLMES. You must avoid the moor in the hours of darkness *at all costs*. It is a landscape that will try to seduce you with its morbid beauty. And you should not leave the house at all without Watson, is that clear?

SIR HENRY. Well I'll try, but I sure don't like bein' pent up.

CONDUCTOR. *(off) All aboard!*

DR. MORTIMER. Shall we proceed, Sir Henry?

HOLMES. Good luck to all of you. Watson.

WATSON. Holmes.

(We hear the opening bars of the Second Movement of Mahler's Symphony Number One in D Major. It's a song of travel.)

Scene Nine: The Train To Baskerville/
Baskerville Station

(We're inside the train carriage with **WATSON**, **DR.**
MORTIMER *and* **SIR HENRY**. **SIR HENRY** *is asleep.*
They sway and bump along with the train.)

WATSON. I looked back at the platform when we had left it
far behind and saw the tall, austere figure of Holmes
standing motionless and gazing after us. I felt alone;
yet I was on my mettle to do my best for Holmes, and
Sir Henry, knowing full well and without regret that
there was danger ahead.

CONDUCTOR. *Grimpen Station! All out for Grimpen!*

SIR HENRY. Hmm? What? What? That was quick.

(WATSON steps out of the train.)

WATSON. Sir. You there in the trap. Could you take us to
Baskerville Hall for a shilling?

TRAP DRIVER. *(ominously)* Baskerville 'All? Are you sure you
wanta go there, young fella?

WATSON. Well yes. I am.

TRAP DRIVER. Fair enough. Climb aboard. If it don't kill ya,
it'll make ya stronger. I believe that's how Nietzsche
puts it, now ain't it. Haw Haw. Don't dawdle ... G'yap.

(Sounds of a clip-clopping horse and trap. WATSON and
SIR HENRY *bounce around in the carriage.)*

WATSON. We proceeded through the moors of Devonshire,
a landscape of such desolation and despair that we
may as well have been visiting another, darker planet
where the limbs, the trunk, the very heart of Nature
were filled with malevolence. My heart grieved for
the world around me; and then I saw it, in its dark,
forbidding glory: Baskerville Hall.

(As they approach Baskerville Hall, the landscape
becomes darker and more threatening. Suddenly, with a
blast of discordant sound, the façade of Baskerville Hall
looms up before them.)

Scene Ten: Baskerville Hall

(WATSON *and* SIR HENRY *walk to the front door of Baskerville Hall, each carrying a suitcase. We hear the "Trauermarsch" [the Funeral March] from the first movement of Mahler's Symphony No. 5 in C Sharp Minor. The Manor House is depressingly glum, the mist is deep and we hear the howls of wolves in the far distance.)*

SIR HENRY. Talk about gloomy. It reminds me of my mama's funeral without the liquor.

WATSON. I'll ring the bell.

(WATSON *pushes the doorbell, and it sounds like the doorbell to hell.)*

(MR. *and* MRS. BARRYMORE *appear.* BARRYMORE *is a hunchback with a withered arm and a full black beard. His wife has a strong Swedish accent, and they are both eerie, indeed mournful in character.)*

BARRYMORE. Good afternoon, sir. Welcome to Baskerville.

MRS. BARRYMORE. Velcome to Baskerwille.

SIR HENRY. You must be Barrymore and the missus. How d'ya do? How d'ya do?

(He shakes their hands and they're aghast.)

I'm Henry, and this is my friend, Doctor Watson. He'll be stayin' here for a while, if that's all right with you.

BARRYMORE. Of course it is, sir. It is your house.

SIR HENRY. I guess that's right. I hadn't thought about it that way. Ha!

MRS. BARRYMORE. Vould you vish der wictuals to be served at vonce, sir?

SIR HENRY. "Der wictuals?"

MRS. BARRYMORE. Ja, der wictuals.

BARRYMORE. The victuals, sir. Your dinner.

SIR HENRY. Oh right! The vittles!

MRS. BARRYMORE. Dere is hot vater in your rooms if you vish to freshen first.

SIR HENRY. Yeah, I think we'll freshen.

BARRYMORE. And may I say that my wife and I will be happy to stay on until you have made arrangements for the new staff.

WATSON. You're leaving?

MRS. BARRYMORE. Vhen it is conwenient, sir.

SIR HENRY. But your family's been here for generations. I'd be sorry to begin my life here by breakin' the connection.

BARRYMORE. We were very attached to Sir Charles, sir, and his untimely death has made these surroundings painful for us. May we show you to your rooms, gentlemen?

(**MRS. BARRYMORE** *picks up* **WATSON***'s suitcase.*)

MRS. BARRMORE. Ve are valking dis vay.

(*walk, walk*)

WATSON. The portraits are beautiful.

MRS. BARRYMORE. Dis vun iss of Sir Hugo Baskerwille, de vun who stole der maiden in der seventeen hondreds. Dey say his neck vas chewed off by de evil hound … Dis is not a good vey to die.

(**WATSON** *reacts and follows her off.*)

Scene Eleven: Watson's Bedroom

(*A bed and a nightstand. A clock is ticking gloomily.*)

(**MRS. BARRYMORE** *leads* **WATSON** *into the room.*)

MRS. BARRYMORE. Da bedwoom.

WATSON. Aha. It's … lovely.

(*She pulls the curtains.*)

MRS. BARRYMORE. Da wiew.

WATSON. Pardon?

MRS. BARRYMORE. Da wiew.

WATSON. Ah yes. The view.

MRS. BARRYMORE. Is vhat I said. Da wista.

WATSON. Of course. The moor. It looks lonely out there. You must be glad to have some company for a change.

MRS. BARRYMORE. Not so much.

(She leaves. WATSON sits on the bed to think. After a moment, he hears the sound of a woman sobbing. He looks up and takes it in. It's heartbreaking.)

WATSON. My dear Holmes. I am sorry for the infrequent bulletins, but I have slept little since arriving at Baskerville Hall.

Scene Twelve: 221B Baker Street

(HOLMES is pacing, reading the letter from WATSON.)

HOLMES. *(overlapping the first sentence with WATSON)* "I am sorry for the infrequent bulletins, but I have slept little since arriving at Baskerville Hall. You know that I am a creature of the Enlightenment and not given to flights of Germanic Romanticism, but for several nights in a row I have heard in the distance the muffled, strangled gasps of one who is torn by an uncontrollable sorrow."

(We hear the sobs again.)

"Meanwhile, Sir Henry remains in surprisingly good spirits – "

SIR HENRY. *(crossing, twirling his six-gun)* Y'all got anything out here I can shoot?

HOLMES. " – and we intend to explore the neighborhood tomorrow morning."

Scene Thirteen: A Path Along the Moors

(The lights come up on a path dappled with bright sunlight. We hear birds twittering, and the world seems brighter. A butterfly appears in the sky.)

*(As it flits through the air, a man (**STAPLETON**) appears with a butterfly net, and he has a tin box for botanical specimens hung over his shoulder. He is about thirty-five, with flaxen hair, wire-rim glasses and a straw hat. He is loveable, cheerful, attractive and eccentric.)*

STAPLETON. *Get back here!!* Shh!! There he is ... I see him ... flutter, flutter ... tip-toe, tip-toe ... raise the net, aaaand ... GYA! Drat! I missed him! I missed him! *Gya – gya – gya – gyaaaa!*

Doctor Watson. Ha, ha.

(calls)

Doctor Watson! Ho!

*(**WATSON** appears.)*

Please excuse my presumption, sir, but Mortimer told me you arrived last week. I'm Stapleton of Merripit House. I live nearby with my sister Beryl.

WATSON. How do you do. You're a naturalist, I hear.

STAPLETON. Yes indeed. Butterflies are my passion.

(miming a catch)

Wsst! Got him! Plunk! Ha! And we're so glad you came! We were all afraid that after the death of poor Sir Charles, the new baronet might refuse to live here. You know about the legend of the hound I suppose.

WATSON. Yes, I've heard it.

STAPLETON. It is *extraordinary* how gullible the locals are about it. Some of them swear that they've actually seen the creature! I have no doubt the story led to Sir Charles's death.

WATSON. How do you mean?

STAPLETON. I saw Sir Charles earlier that day and his nerves were so worked up that the sight of *any* dog would have caused the heart attack. That's my view, but of course the question is what does *Sherlock Holmes* think.

WATSON. ... I beg your pardon?

STAPLETON. Oh come now, it's useless to pretend we don't know you are *the* Doctor Watson. Ha! Even down here we read your *recollections*. And if *you're* here, it follows that Mr. Holmes must be interested in the matter. Am I right? Hmm? When is he coming?

WATSON. I'm afraid I cannot answer that question.

STAPLETON. No of course you can't, but if I can be of any help, just say the word. It's a wonderful place, the moor. You cannot imagine the secrets it contains, so vast and barren. Do you see those bright green spots all scattered round?

WATSON. Yes, they seem more fertile than the rest of it.

STAPLETON. "Fertile?" Ha! That is the great *Grimpen Mire.*

(We hear a blast of discordant music.)

WATSON. "The Grimpen Mire?"

(the sound again)

STAPLETON. One false step means death to man or beast. Only yesterday I saw one of the moor ponies wander into it. He never came out. I saw his head for quite a long time craning out of the bog-hole, then his writhing neck shot upwards and it sucked him down at last.

WATSON. But why do you ever go near the Grimpen Mire?

*(The sound again. **WATSON** is getting a bit tired of it.)*

STAPLETON. Because that is where the *specimens* are, and that's what I do for a ... *wait! Look! It's a Cyclopides!* Excuse me, I'll be right back. Get back here you devil!

(He runs off after the butterfly.)

WATSON. Be careful! You're heading for the Grimp ... the mire! For God's sake man!

*(Suddenly, a **WOMAN** of extraordinary beauty races up the path to **WATSON**. She is clearly distraught, and she grabs him by the arms and shakes him.)*

MISS STAPLETON. *Go back! Go straight back to London instantly!*

WATSON. Wh-why should I go back?

MISS STAPLETON. I can't explain. But for God's sake, do what I ask you.

WATSON. But I've only just come.

MISS STAPLETON. Oh, can't you tell when a warning is for your own good?! Start tonight! Get away from this place at all costs! Shh! Jack is coming. Not a word of what I've just –

(all sweetness and light:)

Hahahaha! Would you mind getting that orchid for me amongst the moor-tails yonder? And oh, just look at that rabbit, isn't he adorable!

(A rabbit goes by.)

STAPLETON. *(entering flushed and panting)* Hello, Beryl!

MISS STAPLETON. Jack, you're so flushed. Did you catch him?

STAPLETON. No, I missed him, blast it! I see you've met our visitor.

MISS STAPLETON. Yes, I was telling Sir Henry that it's rather late for him to see the true beauties of the moor.

STAPLETON. What?

MISS STAPLETON. I said I was telling Sir Henry here that it's getting rather late for –

STAPLETON. Oh, Beryl, this isn't Sir Henry! Ha! You thought it was Sir Hen –

MISS STAPLETON. Oh no!

WATSON. A humble commoner, I'm afraid. How do you do. My name is Watson.

(the ladies' man)

Doctor Watson. General surgeon.

MISS STAPLETON. How do you do. You must think I'm *awfully* silly. We've been talking at cross-purposes.

WATSON. A natural mistake.

STAPLETON. Come, my dear. Let's show the doctor our little abode. We can have some tea to warm us up.

WATSON. May I ask you a question? Why do you live in this part of the world? It's so lonely. Almost primeval.

STAPLETON. We had a school in the north country for a time, but alas, the fates were against us. An epidemic broke out and three of the boys died. There were no accusations, of course, but the school never quite recovered, and much of my capital was swallowed up. With what was left we bought Merripit House and now we're quite fond of the wait ... *wait! There it is again! Shh! It's a Blue Cyclops!* Do you mind if I – ?

(He dashes off.)

I won't be long this time!!

(When **BERYL** *is sure that her brother is gone, she turns to* **WATSON.***)*

MISS STAPLETON. Doctor, I'm sorry to have mistaken you for Sir Henry.

WATSON. Not at all. But why are you so eager to get him away from here?

MISS STAPLETON. I-I know about the curse, that's all ...

WATSON. Please be frank with me, Miss Stapleton. Ever since I've been here I've been conscious of shadows everywhere. This world of yours seems all mud and darkness with no trail to follow and with patches of danger to suck you in.

MISS STAPLETON. *(in despair)* But that's what life is, Doctor. There is nothing else. There is no escape.

*(***MISS STAPLETON** *chokes back a sob. At which moment,* **SIR HENRY** *comes up the path.)*

SIR HENRY. Hello? Doctor Watson? Y'know I get mighty tired of just settin' there doin' paperwork with you out here havin' a good –

(**SIR HENRY** *sees* **MISS STAPLETON** *and is struck dumb with admiration. She, on her side, has the same reaction. It's love at first sight. It's as though there's a piano wire pulled tight between their eyes, tense and resonant, and they simply can't stop staring at each other.* **WATSON** *sees it. He might even wave his hand and get no reaction. Or he might step around the "wire" as if it's really there.* **SIR HENRY** *finally stammers something out:*)

SIR HENRY. Hi. I mean how do you do. My name is oh my lord you have beautiful eyes. I mean, I shouldn't a' said that, should I?

MISS STAPLETON. Oh no! Of course you should! I mean it's quite all right. I'm Miss Stapleton. Beryl. I live here on your mouth. Your moor. I mean the moors. Because they're so beautiful. I'm being silly again.

SIR HENRY. Again? Now when were you ever silly?

MISS STAPLETON. Just a minute ago. I was telling Doctor Watson that you should leave here. But I told *him* to leave because I thought he was you. But he isn't you, is he?

SIR HENRY. No he's not.

WATSON. She was very upset. She insisted.

MISS STAPLETON. You make too much of it, Doctor. My brother and I were shocked by the death of Sir Charles, so when his heir came to live here, I became distressed.

SIR HENRY. *(happily)* You were distressed for me?

MISS STAPLETON. Yes, I was. I am. You must go away for your own sake. Why live in a place that has been fatal to your family, a place of danger?

SIR HENRY. Because it *is* a place of danger. That makes life interestin'. Besides, maybe now it's a place of somethin' else. Or am I mistaken?

MISS STAPLETON. No. I think you are not mistaken. And yet it's foolish! You should go back while you have the chance! The danger here is *very real* and it's not something to laugh off because of momentary feelings of –

(Suddenly, there is a howl in the distance and they all look up. It's a long, low moan, incredibly sad. Then it swells into a deep, almost satanic roar. MISS STAPLETON *turns pale.)*

There it is. That's the hound.

(The hound cries out again and its hideous howl echoes across the moors.)

It never stops! It howls and cries and brings nothing but death!

(It continues to howl and she becomes hysterical.)

It's not a myth, it can hurt people and kill them and make them suffer!

SIR HENRY. Beryl!

WATSON. Miss Stapleton!

MISS STAPLETON. *Go back! Please listen to me! Save yourself! I beg of you! You'll be killed!*

(Another horrible howl and MISS STAPLETON *screams and faints dead away in* SIR HENRY*'s arms.* WATSON *and* SIR HENRY *are dumbfounded.)*

(The jangled tonalities of the Dies Irae from Benjamin Britten's War Requiem *take us straight into:)*

Scene Fourteen: 221B Baker Street

HOLMES. *Cartwright! Milker!*

*(*HOLMES *is sitting in a chair with his back to us.)*

CARTWRIGHT. *(off)* We're right 'ere, sir! We're on the way up!

*(*MILKER *enters without* CARTWRIGHT*.)*

HOLMES. Do you have the letter?!

MILKER. Yes we do, sir!

HOLMES. Then what are you waiting for? Christmas?! Get up here!

CARTWRIGHT. *(rushing in, disheveled)* Here I am, sir! I'm right here! (one on each side of him, me on right)

HOLMES. What took you so long?!

CARTWRIGHT. *(the actor)* You have no idea …

HOLMES. Now first of all, what happened with *The Times*? Did you find the copy with the cut-out letters?

MILKER. No sir. No luck. But we did have fun lookin' through all that trash.

HOLMES. As I suspected. Now read me Doctor Watson's letter. And curse my experiments, curse explosives and curse the day *I ever needed eyes in the first place!!*

(He rises and turns and we see that his eyes are bandaged.) (push him down)

CARTWRIGHT. You get them bandages off tomorrow, don't ya?

HOLMES. That or I'll strangle the doctor who put them on me, now read! (push him down) (make self at home)

(CARTWRIGHT tears the letter open and looks at it.)

CARTWRIGHT. Whoops. It ain't from Doctor Watson after all, it's from one o' your many, many beautiful girlfriends, in fact I think it's that tall blonde one with the silky hair and the …

(HOLMES is unamused.)

HOLMES. Is this your idea of humor, Cartwright?

CARTWRIGHT. *(gulp)* Yeah, it was.

HOLMES. Well it was very poor.

CARTWRIGHT. Sorry. Ahem. "From Doctor John Watson to Mr. Sherlock 'Olmes, My dear 'Olmes. My previous letters have kept you pretty well up-to-date so far, but there is a new development to add to the mosaic that you and I are so carefully assembling." 'E's a very good writer.

(explore when he takes letter)

MILKER. *(grabbing the letter)* My turn! "Our friend Sir Henry begins to display a considerable interest in our neighbor, Miss Stapleton. It is not to be wondered at, for she is a very fascinating and beautiful woman." Ugh! It's revolting.

CARTWRIGHT. *(grabbing the letter back)* "There is something quite exotic about her, and Sir Henry says she has hidden fires buried deep inside her bosom."

MILKER. *Bosom! Haaaa!*

CARTWRIGHT. Bosom! *(fall into seat laughing)*

(They carry on, delighted by the word 'bosom.')

HOLMES. That's it! That's it! I can stand it no longer!

CARTWRIGHT. *Mr. 'Olmes!* *(scared and jump up quickly)*

HOLMES. *Eyes! Eyes! I need my eyes!*

MILKER. But Mr. 'Olmes!

HOLMES. *(untangling) They are 'kin to my soul and must be fed or else I wither like the stalk of summer!*

(He tears the bandages off in a fury of frustration.)

CARTWRIGHT. Sir!

HOLMES. *Now where's the letter?!*

(MILKER, his hand shaking, offers the letter. HOLMES snatches it and glares at the paper, adjusting his eyes with great effort to the light and the writing.)

Thank you. " … buried deep inside her bosom."

(The boys start to laugh again but HOLMES stops them.)

"There is more important news, however. When I was out one night last week I caught a glimpse of someone whom I could not identify as one of the villagers. He was silhouetted in the moonlight and I could see his wiry figure standing quite still at first, then capering over the rocks like a sprite. I have begun to think of him as the Man of Mystery." How curious.

CARTWRIGHT. Yeah, it's curious all right.

MILKER. Very curious.

CARTWRIGHT. Gives me curiosity.

MILKER. And wonder.

CARTWRIGHT. And surprise.

MILKER. And amazement. *[Get up quickly and start to move stage left.]*

HOLMES. *That's enough.* "I saw the man from a distance several nights in a row, but I have not seen him for the past two days. He comes and goes and seems to melt, almost magically, into the landscape." Watson. He is our better self.

"And now let me tell you more about the Barrymores."

(The BOYS don't react. HOLMES [the actor] tries again: The BOYS need time to change costumes.)

"The Barrymores."

(The BOYS get it and run off as fast as they can.)

"The surprising development began last night. As you know, I am a very sound sleeper, but at two in the morning I was aroused by a stealthy step passing my room."

(We see the following acted out by WATSON.)

"I got out of bed and saw a shadow in the hall, a man going by, or so I thought. My instinct was to follow him alone, but I thought better of it and crept into Sir Henry's room down the corridor and woke him quietly."

Scene Fifteen: The Upstairs Rooms of Baskerville Hall

WATSON. *(whispering)* Sir Henry, wake up …

SIR HENRY. *(starting up from his bed, frightened, holding a gun)* What?! What is it?!!

WATSON. Shhh! Shhh!

SIR HENRY. Holy cow! I thought I was bein' murdered in my bed like my Uncle Willie.

WATSON. Something strange is occurring. Follow me.

SIR HENRY. You got it!

(*SIR HENRY follows* **WATSON** *into the corridor.*)

(*They enter a large room with a window overlooking the moor. A shadowy* **MAN** *at the window lights a match — and we see that it's* **BARRYMORE**. *He lights a candle from the match, then kneels in front of the window. Then he raises the candle up and down, then side to side, as if signaling someone in the distance.*)

SIR HENRY. (*gun in hand*) Barrymore!

BARRYMORE. (*leaping in fright*) Agh!

SIR HENRY. *What are you doin'?!*

BARRYMORE. *I was looking for Russia!*

SIR HENRY. Oh baloney! Now listen, Barrymore, I want the truth out of you, *now what were you doin' at that window?!*

BARRYMORE. *Don't ask me, Sir Henry! Please! I give you my word that it is not my secret!*

WATSON. Wait a moment, I have an idea.

(*He takes the candle and he holds it up to the window.*)

He must have been signaling someone. Let's see if there's an answer.

(*He lifts the candle up and down, then peers out into the darkness. There's a pause, and then in the far distance we see a pinpoint of light signaling back.*)

There! There it is! An answering light! Out on the moor!

SIR HENRY. (*agitated*) Now you wretch, do you deny it's a signal?! Who's that out yonder and what's goin' on?! *Tell me! TELL ME RIGHT NOW!*

(**MRS. BARRYMORE** *appears dramatically in the doorway and cries out.*)

MRS. BARRYMORE. *HE CANNOT TELL YOU!*

BARRYMORE. *Inga!*

MRS. BARRYMORE. *It iss my brudder!* My brudder iss starwing on de moor! Der light is a signal dat wictuals is ready for him, and his light iss to show us vhere to bring dem.

WATSON. Then your brother is

MRS. BARRYMORE. *(weeping)* His name is Wictor. He iss a conwict.

WATSON. Pardon?

MRS. BARRYMORE. *(weeping)* A *conwict.*

(**WATSON** *and* **SIR HENRY** *are still confused.*)

He vas incarserwated.

SIR HENRY. What?

MRS. BARRYMORE. He vas awwested, he vas in pwison!

BARRYMORE. He was in *jail!*

(She weeps uncontrollably.)

MRS. BARRYMORE. He iss my younger brudder. He vas a good boy, but I could never enwision vhat is going to happen to him. As he gwew older he met vicked conwict companions and vent fwom wictum to wictum like a wicious dog *und he broke our hearts!* He iss starwing out dhere in de svamp, und I send him prowisions und clothing. Sir Henwy, vhen you threw out your old clothing last veek, I gave dem to Wictor. I am wery sowwy!

SIR HENRY. Oh that's all right. And I can't say I fault you, Barrymore, for standin' by your wife. We'll discuss it in the mornin'.

MRS. BARRYMORE. Wery goot, sir.

BARRYMORE. Very good, sir.

(**BARRYMORE** *leads his wife, still weeping, out the door.* **SIR HENRY** *stares out the window at the pinpoint of light, which is still visible. He's itching to run out and find the man.*)

SIR HENRY. Just look at that light out there. And he's a convict! How far out there do you think he is?

WATSON. It can't be too far if they carried provisions out to him.

SIR HENRY. The dirty villain, with that candle o' his.

(*He pulls his gun.*)

This is *my* castle! C'mon! Let's go take him!

WATSON. I agree!

(*Adventurous music begins thumping away. It might be the opening of Act II, Scene 2 of Verdi's* Don Carlo.)

Scene Sixteen: The Moors at Night

(**WATSON** *and* **SIR HENRY** *rush on, each carrying a pistol. Clouds drive over the face of the sky, the moon shedding steel grey light over the decaying moors. Huge stones dot the landscape, with many places for a man to hide, and the wind blows ferociously.*)

SIR HENRY. It's dark out here.

WATSON. We should close on him rapidly. I'm sure he'll be desperate.

SIR HENRY. I wonder what Holmes would say about this? Ha!

(*At which moment, we hear the howl of the hound as we heard it before, but in the darkness and the shadows, the sound takes on an even greater sense of foreboding and terror. The creature moans, then cries out, and the sound echoes across the landscape.*)

Good God ... D'ya think there's any truth to them stories?

WATSON. I ... no. I don't believe it. I have lived my life believing that the world is rational. It has to be.

(*another howl*)

SIR HENRY. But that sound, it just ... my hands are freezin'.

WATSON. Shall we turn back?

SIR HENRY. No! I won't do it! We're after a convict and I
ain't lettin' some ol' hound dog stop me!

WATSON. Wait! Look! It's a candle stuck in the rock. We
must be close!

(At this moment, from behind the boulder, VICTOR
*appears. He has an evil yellow face, seamed and scored
with vile passions. He rears up with a roar.)*

SIR HENRY. Victor!

*(He's a brute of a man, huge and muscular, in tattered
rags, filthy from the mire. The* MEN *cry out and go for
their weapons, but it's too late.)*

VICTOR. *Noooo! Leave me alone! It iss not your business! I vill
have my wengeance! Go avay! Go avay!*

(The brute lashes out and knocks SIR HENRY *several
yards away.* WATSON *jumps on the* MAN *and they
struggle, but* WATSON *is no match for the giant. He
strikes* WATSON *and* WATSON *staggers backward.* SIR
HENRY *is trying to reach for his revolver and* VICTOR
sees it. He kicks the gun out of SIR HENRY'S *hand.*
WATSON *is now trying to stand up. This time* VICTOR
grabs a huge rock and strikes WATSON *on the head with
it.* WATSON *cries out in pain, falls to the ground and
loses consciousness.)*

SIR HENRY. *Watson!*

*(*VICTOR *runs away with a cry as* SIR HENRY *races to*
WATSON'S *side. He lifts* WATSON'S *head but there is no
life in it.)*

*(*SIR HENRY *can barely speak.)*

Oh my God. He's dead. Help! Help! Somebody help!
Doctor Watson is dead!

End of Act One

ACT TWO

Scene One: The Moors, then the Sitting Room at Baskerville Hall

*(Fierce, exciting music. The opening moment is a replay of the end of Act One. We're on the moors just as **VICTOR** grabs the rock, then rushes to **WATSON** and strikes him with it. **WATSON** cries out in pain, falls to the ground and loses consciousness.)*

SIR HENRY. *Watson!*

*(VICTOR runs away with a cry as **SIR HENRY** races to **WATSON**'s side. He lifts **WATSON**'s head but there is no life in it. **SIR HENRY** can barely speak.)*

Oh my God. He's dead. Help! Help! Somebody help! *Doctor Watson is dead!*

*(**SIR HENRY** fades away and so does the moor. We see **WATSON** lying dead on the ground. Then he sits up and looks at the audience:)*

WATSON. I was not dead. I was, however, deeply humiliated. Sir Henry carried me back to the manor where I was attended by a doctor named Hamish McCann and his nurse, a Miss Malloy.

*(We are in the sitting room at Baskerville Hall and the **DOCTOR** and **NURSE** are in attendance. They have broad accents, Scots and Irish respectively.)*

DOCTOR MCCANN. As your doctor, let me say this could have been much worse. Your skull appears to be abnormally thick.

WATSON. That's what Holmes says.

DOCTOR MCCANN. Rest up for a few days, you'll be as good as new.

(*He exits. The extremely attractive nurse stays and adjusts* WATSON*'s bandage.*)

WATSON. *Ow!*

NURSE MALLOY. Your pardon, kind sir, I was tryin' to adjust this wicked bandage.

WATSON. *(testy)* Well in the future, would you be so kind as to – !

(*He sees that she's a knock-out.*)

Oh, hello. You did that beautifully.

NURSE MALLOY. Thank you, sir. It's quite a wound and'll take some healin'. Shall I sit with you while you rest, sir?

WATSON. Yes that would be lovely. I'd like that.

NURSE MALLOY. *(taking his hand)* There now, you just close them eyes. I'm right here.

(**NURSE MALLOY** *sits next to* **WATSON** *and strokes his hand.* **WATSON***'s eyes are closed and he sighs happily. After a beat,* **HOLMES** *walks in silently.* **NURSE MALLOY** *sees him and is about to speak, but* **HOLMES** *puts his finger to his lips to keep her silent. He hands her a pound note and motions for her to leave the room. She gets up – and* **HOLMES** *takes* **WATSON***'s hand and sits where the* **NURSE** *was sitting. The transition is seamless.* **NURSE MALLOY** *disappears.* **HOLMES** *pats* **WATSON***'s hand.* **WATSON** *sighs happily again.*)

WATSON. This really is quite refreshing.

HOLMES. I'm not surprised.

WATSON. *Holmes!*

(*He springs up.*)

What are you – ?! How did you – ?!

HOLMES. Just checking up on you, Watson.

WATSON. I'm fine!

HOLMES. You are not fine. As I understand it, you were almost killed by that brute on the moor. Perhaps you should leave the case entirely. It's getting too dangerous.

WATSON. Never! I intend to see it to the end.

HOLMES. There are layers here, Watson! Layers on layers and nothing adds up.

*(During the following description of suspects, the characters appear in a passing dumbshow, acting out the characters that **HOLMES** is creating for them. This is continuous and does not slow down the flow of the narrative.)*

On the one hand, there's this Victor fellow who's obviously violent but comes out of the blue.

*(**VICTOR** crosses.)*

VICTOR. *(to the audience)* Supwise.

HOLMES. Yet he is connected to the Baskervilles through his sister, and I suppose there might have been a liaison between Sir Charles and Mrs. Barrymore which Victor is out to exploit or revenge …

*(**SIR CHARLES** and **MRS. BARRYMORE** appear and put roses in their teeth and dance off.)*

WATSON. With Mrs. Barrymore? Oh I doubt it. She's like something out of *Frankenstein*.

HOLMES. You would be surprised. Then there's Barrymore *husband*,

*(**MR. BARRYMORE** hobbles in with a large, nasty knife –)*

who sounds peculiar, but is harmless as far as I can see.

(– and then harmlessly cuts an apple with it.)

Of course if his wife and Sir Charles did have an affair, he might have killed Sir Charles out of revenge, but that shouldn't threaten Sir Henry.

*(**SIR HENRY** crosses –)*

unless this Barrymore is a maniac,

(– and **BARRYMORE** *pursues* **SIR HENRY** *with a hatchet.*)

HOLMES. *(cont.)* which is not impossible. And then there's Stapleton, who's obviously mad as a hatter

(On hearing the word "Stapleton," the **ACTOR** *stops and changes costume from* **BARRYMORE** *to* **STAPLETON** *in front of the audience – including a butterfly net thrown in from the wings and caught expertly.)*

but has nothing to gain as far as I can see; and his sister, Beryl, who could be the worst of the lot and is simply pretending to be the soul of innocence.

WATSON. Don't tell Sir Henry that. He's besotted with her.

*(***BERYL** *and* **SIR HENRY** *waltz in.)*

HOLMES. All the more reason to worry about her, she could be using him to get the money.

SIR HENRY. *(overhearing this)* Huh?

(She yanks him offstage. The dumbshow is over.)

HOLMES. Has anything else turned up? Any sign of the hound?

WATSON. None. But you know that Man of Mystery I wrote you about? I saw him up close the other night.

HOLMES. *(surprised)* You did?

WATSON. Yes. I was taking a final look round the grounds before going to bed and there he was, standing on the rocks at the back.

(We see the outline of the **MAN OF MYSTERY** *cross at the back.)*

He comes and goes at will, like a phantom.

HOLMES. Is he anything like our friend Victor?

WATSON. No, no. Different type entirely. This fellow seems older and slightly out of his head from the way he mutters and gibbers and shambles along. When you see him I'm sure you'll learn a great deal more.

HOLMES. Well I won't, I'm afraid.

WATSON. Why not?

HOLMES. Because I'm leaving.

WATSON. What? Again? You can't!

HOLMES. I'm sorry.

WATSON. But Holmes – !

HOLMES. I can't possibly stay. Press of work, the Bohemia business.

WATSON. But you just arrived!

HOLMES. I'm sorry.

WATSON. Have you seen Sir Henry at least?

HOLMES. No no, I don't want to. He'll make a fuss. I just wanted to make sure you weren't dead or something.

WATSON. Well I'm not.

HOLMES. Apparently. Now listen closely. I want you to stay and keep me informed. And you must keep a closer eye on Sir Henry.

WATSON. Right.

SIR HENRY. *(off) Hey, Doctor!*

WATSON. There he is.

HOLMES. All yours.

WATSON. Now Holmes, just wait a moment –

SIR HENRY. *(off) Doctor!*

WATSON. I'm coming, I'm coming!

(He turns but **HOLMES** *is gone.)*

Holmes? Holmes – ?!

*(***SIR HENRY*** *enters, passing* **WATSON** *as he heads for the front door of the mansion.)*

SIR HENRY. Hey Doctor, I'll see ya later. I'm just goin' out by myself for a spell. To tell you the truth, I'm goin' out to meet Beryl.

WATSON. Oh no you're not.

SIR HENRY. Oh yes I am.

WATSON. *Stop. Sir Henry, stop!* You know what Holmes said: You may not go out onto the moors unaccompanied and that is final!

SIR HENRY. Listen, I've got two answers for you. First of all, we've been through a lot together, so you've got to stop callin' me *Sir* Henry. My name's Henry, and I'll call you Johnny.

WATSON. John.

SIR HENRY. Okay. John-Boy. Or Bubba.

WATSON. John-Boy.

SIR HENRY. You got it. Second of all, Mr. Holmes in all his wisdom did not foresee certain romantic developments which have transpired since I've been here, and I'm sure you ain't a spoil-sport, right? Now take a nap and I'll see ya later.

WATSON. No. Stop. Stop! Would you please – !

STAPLETON. *(from the next scene)* Don't move!

Scene Two: A Path on the Moors

(It's a beautiful day, and we hear birds twittering in the bright sunlight. STAPLETON has run on with his butterfly net and is wearing his related paraphernalia.)

STAPLETON. *Stop!*

(The butterfly alghts and he creeps up on it.)

You have been tempting me like a French can-can dancer for over a week, now prepare to meet your makerrrrrgya!! Gya! Gya!

*(He runs off, then **BERYL** hurries on. She looks stunning.)*

MISS STAPLETON. Henry … ? *Henry … ?*

SIR HENRY. *(entering) Beryl!*

MISS STAPLETON. *(embracing him joyfully)* Oh, Henry, I've missed you so much!

SIR HENRY. It's only been a day, you know. And you still look beautiful.

MISS STAPLETON. You spoil me terribly.

SIR HENRY. Good, 'cause I mean to. Now listen, I've been thinkin' about a lot of things.

MISS STAPLETON. That's excellent. I hear that thinking is very good for the brain.

SIR HENRY. You're makin' fun of me.

MISS STAPLETON. Just a little. You are from Texas.

SIR HENRY. And you live in a swamp.

MISS STAPLETON. It's not a swamp, it's a moor. And at least we don't have crocodiles and kangaroos.

SIR HENRY. That's Australia.

MISS STAPLETON. Oh. Right. I get the colonies mixed up sometimes. They all seem to have cowboys and uprisings and

SIR HENRY. Miss Stapleton! You are interruptin' my interruptions and I want to say my piece.

MISS STAPLETON. Oh all right, I suppose you're allowed to talk now and then.

SIR HENRY. Good, because I want to marry you.

(*Beat. Her mouth drops open. She's speechless, then erupts with shock and joy and distress.*)

MISS STAPLETON. Oh my God. I never thought … Oh, *yes.* I'd go anywhere in the world with you! But you'll have to promise me we'll leave this place. We'll go together. We can't stay here. It's a place of danger. Oh!

(*She's overcome with the thought of it. She kisses him passionately. At which moment,* **STAPLETON** *enters.*)

STAPLETON. Beryl … Beryl?

(*He hasn't expected to see what he's seeing and he stops dead. His face goes white and he drops his butterfly net. He's in shock.*)

How – how dare you. *How dare you!*

(*He turns red with fury and almost dances in place.*)

Sir! What do you think you are doing?! That is my … SISTER! Do you think you can just … walk into Baskerville Hall and just TAKE HER AWAY! Because you're a BARONET?!!

MISS STAPLETON. *Jack, for God's sake!*

SIR HENRY. *(amazed)* Let me assure you, sir, that my intentions are honorable.

STAPLETON. *Honorable?!*

SIR HENRY. In fact, I've asked your sister to marry me.

STAPLETON. Marr – ? *Beryl! Get over here! Right now!*

(**SIR HENRY** *puts a protective arm around* **BERYL.**)

SIR HENRY. Now listen here! You have no right to speak to her like that and I'm not gonna – !

STAPLETON. Speak to her? Have you – ? Are you – ? *Beryl!*

(**BERYL** *goes to her* **BROTHER,** *her head bent.*)

SIR HENRY. *(really losing his temper)* You *hound dog!! Leave her alone!*

MISS STAPLETON. No! Henry! It's all right. Just leave it. It's hopeless.

STAPLETON. *Beryl!* Come with me.

(to **SIR HENRY***)*

I shall speak to you later … *Sir!*

(**STAPLETON** *marches* **BERYL** *off.* **SIR HENRY** *watches them go in amazement – as* **WATSON** *enters down the lane.*)

SIR HENRY. Holy cow. You should have seen what just –

WATSON. I did. I saw all of it. I hated to spy on you, dear fellow, but I thought it better if he didn't see me.

SIR HENRY. Oh that's all right. But why in the world would he act like that? Do you think he's crazy?

WATSON. I suppose it's possible.

SIR HENRY. I think he needs a *straitjacket.* I mean what's he got against me? I got plenty of money and I never hurt anybody.

STAPLETON. *(off)* Sir Henry.

WATSON. *(hiding behind a rock)* Sh! Don't say a word!

(STAPLETON *re-enters. He has attempted to calm down and he looks ashamed of himself, but his heart is still racing and he speaks with difficulty.*)

(BERYL *is with him. But it's clear that she is cowed by* STAPLETON, *and she remains silent.*)

(SIR HENRY *instinctively pulls himself into a fighting stance.*)

Please, sir. I've come to apologize. I suppose I overreacted.

SIR HENRY. You suppose that do ya?

STAPLETON. You must understand ... my sister is everything to me. We've been together – just the two of us – since we were children, and I had no idea that you two had ... fallen in love. I do apologize. I'm deeply sorry.

SIR HENRY. Well, that's very handsome of ya.

STAPLETON. Perhaps you could dine with us this Friday. I could make amends. But I must ask you one thing, even now, and that is to please let matters rest till then so that I can get used to the idea – at which time I will withdraw any opposition to the match without hesitation. That is a promise.

SIR HENRY. Well. I suppose a few days ain't too bad.

STAPLETON. So we'll see you Friday then. Good-bye.

MISS STAPLETON. Good-bye, Henry.

(*A roll of thunder and the stage darkens.*)

WATSON. *(a letter)* It was now, dear Holmes, that events began crowding thick and fast upon us, and I soon had the feeling that our lives were hurtling without control towards a remarkable and inevitable conclusion. The fuse was lit by Mrs. Barrymore.

Scene Three: Baskerville Hall

(Thunder. **MRS. BARRYMORE** *is speaking to* **SIR HENRY** *and* **WATSON**. *In her excitement, her Swedish accent is more pronounced than ever.)*

MRS. BARRYMORE. *(passionately)* I must speak vith you, Sir Henry! It is wital!

BARRYMORE. *(entering)* Inga, you need not tell them!

MRS. BARRYMORE. But I must!

WATSON. Please, Mrs. Barrymore. Go ahead.

SIR HENRY. We're listenin'.

MRS. BARRYMORE. You und Doctor Vatson haff been wery kind to us und ve thought ve should tell you: ve do know something inwolving the wiolent death of Sir Charles.

SIR HENRY. Ya mean ya know how he died?!

BARRYMORE. Not precisely, sir, but we do know why he was at the gate at that time of night.

MRS. BARRYMORE. It vas a wigil to meet a vooman.

WATSON. Who was she?

BARRYMORE. We don't know her name, sir.

MRS. BARRYMORE. But her initials vas "L.L."

BARRYMORE. *(to* **SIR HENRY***)* You see, your uncle Charles had a letter the morning he was killed, and I saw that it was a woman's writing. I told Inga about it.

MRS. BARRYMORE. Und I do not think again of it for veeks und veeks, but then, when I vas cleaning out Sir Charles's study, I found der *ashes* of a *burned letter* at der back of der *grate*. Most of it vas charred to pieces, but *vone piece* at der end of der letter vas hanging together like little precious paper babies holding hands and I could read der writings. It said

(We see a projection of the letter behind the **MEN** *as* **MRS. BARRYMORE** *reads:)*

"Please, please, as you are a gentleman, burn this letter, and be at the gate by ten o'clock. I feel so wulnerable. L.L."

(See Appendix for the letter as it should appear. If there is no projection, MRS. BARRYMORE should not say "I feel so vulnerable." Those four words should be dropped.)

SIR HENRY. Have you got the slip?

MRS. BARRYMORE. No, sir. Der babies crumble as I moved dem.

WATSON. And you have no idea who "L.L." is?

BARRYMORE. We do not know that, sir.

MRS. BARRYMORE. But if you find der lady, you vill learn things, ja?

SIR HENRY. Did Sir Charles have a lot of lady friends? Or "girlfriends" you might say?

MRS. BARRYMORE. *(scandalized, indignant)* "Girlfriends?!" Oh no, sir! *He vas over fifty!*

BARRYMORE. May we go now, sir?

SIR HENRY. O'course you may.

MRS. BARRYMORE. Fifty years old.

BARRYMORE. "Girlfriends."

MRS. BARRYMORE. I could womit.

(They're gone.)

WATSON. "L.L."

SIR HENRY. Does that strike a bell with you?

WATSON. I'm afraid not.

SIR HENRY. Me neither.

WATSON. We need someone who's acquainted with everyone in the district.

(They look at each other.)

SIR HENRY/WATSON. Doctor Mortimer!

SIR HENRY. *Let's go!*

(They hurry to the front door of the manor. When they pull it open, the blast of the howling wind blows them backwards. But they pull themselves together and fight their way out the door and into:)

Scene Four: A Street in Coombe Tracy

(WATSON *and* SIR HENRY *are fighting their way against
the wind. Their scarves billow out behind them and they
hold their hats. They have to shout to each other to be
heard.*)

WATSON. *I think he lives around here someplace!*

(WINNIE, *a young mother pushing a baby carriage is
also on the street, walking in the same direction as the
two* MEN. *She's fighting the wind as hard as they are,
pushing the carriage in front of her with all her might.
To their consternation, she passes them and keeps on
going.*)

SIR HENRY. *Wait! There he is! Doctor Mortimer!*

WATSON. *We need to speak to you!*

DR. MORTIMER. *(equally buffeted and shouting) I'm heading
home, where are you two going?!*

SIR HENRY. *To your house! We wanted to ask you somethin'!*

DR. MORTIMER. *Well go ahead!*

(*They all plod along the street, fighting the wind.*)

SIR HENRY. *We're lookin' for a woman with the initials "L.L."!*

DR. MORTIMER. *What?!*

WATSON. *We're looking for a woman!*

DR. MORTIMER. *So am I! I'm tired of being single!*

WATSON. *No! A special woman!*

DR. MORTIMER. *Me, too! They're hard to find around here!*

SIR HENRY. *No, no, listen! We have a clue!*

DR. MORTIMER. *Why do you need glue?*

WATSON. *What?!*

DR. MORTIMER. *I don't have any glue!*

WATSON. *We're looking for a woman so we can ask her some
questions!!*

DR. MORTIMER. *In my case, it's to have children! Shall we go
inside?!*

(They go into **DR. MORTIMER***'s house and slam the door behind them, panting from the wind.)*

Scene Five: Dr. Mortimer's House and Office

DR. MORTIMER. How's the case coming along?

WATSON. Well at the moment we're looking for a woman in the district with the initials "L.L."

DR. MORTIMER. There's only one as far as I know. Her name is Laura Lyons. She has a typing establishment on Front Street, just down the road. She married against her family's wishes, the man deserted her, and now she desperately needs money for a divorce.

WATSON. How terribly sad.

DR. MORTIMER. Wait a moment! There he is again!

WATSON. Who?!

*(***DR. MORTIMER*** snatches a telescope from his desk and peers through the window.)*

DR. MORTIMER. I've seen a man out there on the rocks, watching everything in the village.

WATSON. The Man of Mystery!

SIR HENRY. Where does he live, do you reckon?

DR. MORTIMER. I don't reckon, I know. I've spotted him at the Black Tor. It's that rocky area with the hill above it. He's living in one of those stone huts.

*(***DR. MORTIMER***'s nurse,* **NURSE MACKEEBLE***, runs in.)*

NURSE MACKEEBLE. Doctor Mortimer, y'have patients waitin'! I canna hold 'em off much longer!

DR. MORTIMER. Excuse me, gentlemen. I've got to run.

(And without warning, he tears out, running as fast as he can.)

NURSE MACKEEBLE. *(following him off)* He's on his way so hold your pants together!

WATSON. The Black Tor.

SIR HENRY. He's hidin' out there and I don't like it.

WATSON. I'd like to confront him.

SIR HENRY. I'd like to do more than that!

(*They look at each other.*)

So what are we waitin' for?

WATSON. Let's go!

(*They clatter down the steps, then out the door, and the wind on the street hits them again, harder than ever.*)

Scene Six: The Black Tor

(*They're on the Black Tor, at the summit of a steep hill. Below them there is a clearing with several crude, makeshift stone huts.*)

SIR HENRY. (*looking down*) It didn't look this high from Dr. Mortimer's window.

WATSON. I can see the hut down there at the bottom.

(*A very, very old* **COUNTRY FARMER** *hobbles by, pulling one of his sheep on a leash as he goes. When he speaks, he whistles.*)

COUNTRY FARMER. Now watch your step, young fellas. It can get pretty slippery way up here on a night like this.

SIR HENRY. Thanks, old fella, but I'm used to bein' on hills like this in Texas and I never slip down this kinda grouaaaaaaaaa …

WATSON/SIR HENRY. Ahhh!

(*Both* **MEN** *lose their footing and slide down the hill into the clearing. They land on their backsides, then pick themselves up. We see a stone hut nearby.*)

SIR HENRY. Are you all right?

WATSON. Fine. Look. There's the hut. It still has a roof on it.

SIR HENRY. There's nobody inside. Come on.

(The MEN *enter the hut and grope through it in the half-light.)*

SIR HENRY. There ain't no question that somebody lives here. Look at this: blankets. Canned peaches.

WATSON. What's this? It looks like a diary of some kind.

(He picks up a piece of paper from the table and peers at it in the darkness. Reading:)

It says "Three forty-two p.m. Doctor Watson and Sir Henry have gone to see … *have gone to see Doctor Mortimer." Good heavens!*

(Immediately the tension ratchets up. Foreboding music starts to play. WATSON *is dumbfounded.)*

WATSON. What is this? What's going on?

SIR HENRY. We're bein' followed, and they've gotta be mighty close by. I'll go find 'em.

(He takes out his revolver.)

WATSON. All right. But be careful.

*(*SIR HENRY *exits the hut, then exits the clearing.* WATSON *is upset. He looks at the report, then reads more of it.)*

"As noted earlier, Doctor Mortimer lives at the end of town, and I would guess that they plan to question him regarding Laura Lyons – !"

(Snap!)

(A twig snaps outside the hut. Someone is approaching. WATSON *takes out his service revolver and steps into the shadows.)*

(Snap!)

(The MAN OF MYSTERY *enters the clearing, stealthily, and senses that someone is in his hut. He draws a pistol. Then he sniffs the air and smiles. He recognizes the scent.)*

MAN OF MYSTERY. *(calling)* Come out o' there young man or there's gonna be trouble!

*(*WATSON *springs out of the hut, gun raised.)*

WATSON. *Stay where you are! I have you covered!*

MAN OF MYSTERY. *You're covered as well!*

(The two **MEN** *are facing each other with their firearms raised.)*

Now what'll it be?! Death for one of us –

(Using his own – **HOLMES**'s *– voice:)*

or shall we settle it over a nice cup of tea, my dear Watson?

WATSON. *(shocked)* Holmes?

HOLMES. Hello, dear fellow.

(He pulls his wig off.)

WATSON. Was it you all along?

HOLMES. I'm afraid it was. And I'm glad you applied your usual, pungent shaving cream this morning, or I wouldn't have known it was you in the hut.

WATSON. Oh my dear Holmes, it's good to see you!

(He wrings his friend's hand with joy and relief. During the following, **HOLMES** *removes his disguise and returns to his cat-like self.)*

HOLMES. I didn't expect you to find me this soon.

WATSON. Dr. Mortimer spotted you scrambling on the rocks.

HOLMES. And you've just been to see him – to find Laura Lyons, I imagine?

WATSON. Yes, but what are you doing here?! I thought you were in Baker Street working on that blackmailing case.

HOLMES. That's what I wished you to think. I thought if the two of us could explore the case independently, from different angles, we could make more progress. At the moment, I'm trying to track down this Mrs. Lyons.

WATSON. Well I think I've done it. Mortimer says she lives down on Front Street.

HOLMES. Oh excellent, Watson! Well done! Good man! You're getting better than I am at this detective business. I'll have to take up doctoring soon.

WATSON. (*pleased*) Oh I say …

HOLMES. Your next move, I take it, is to see Mrs. Lyons.

WATSON. Exactly.

HOLMES. Then we'll go together. You *are* aware that a close intimacy exists between Mrs. Lyons and the man Stapleton.

WATSON. No I'm not.

HOLMES. They meet, they write, and I think we can use it to detach him from his wife so we can question her.

WATSON. … His wife? You mean Stapleton's wife? I didn't know he had one.

HOLMES. The woman Beryl who passes as his sister is in fact his wife. I believe he forces her into it.

WATSON. What?! That's shocking! You mean then – ?

HOLMES. *He* is our enemy. Stapleton. He *must* be! There is no other calculus that makes sense.

WATSON. But how do you know that she *is* his wife?

HOLMES. Because he forgot himself! I did some sleuthing in *The Times* archives and learned that a school in the North did indeed come to grief under the atrocious circumstances he described, and that the man who owned the school disappeared with his *wife*. I'm hoping to receive a photograph soon to confirm his identity.

VOICE. (*off*) *AAAAAAAAAAAAHHHHHHHHHHHHHHHHH HHHH!!!!!!!!*

(*It's a scream of horror and anguish from a voice in such distress that it's unrecognizable. Both men freeze.*)

WATSON. *Oh my God! What is it?! What could be –*

HOLMES. *Hush!*

VOICE. *(off) AAAAAAAAAAAAHHHHHHHHHHHHHHHHH HHHH!!!!!!!!*

HOLMES. *Where is it, Watson?! Where is it?!*

WATSON. *There, I think!*

HOUND. *(off)* REOOOOOW! ROOOOOOAAUUGHH!

(A new sound has joined the first: the sound of a giant hound crying out and snarling.)

WATSON. *The hound! It's the hound! Come quickly, Holmes!*

(They rush through the moor, this way and that, trying to follow the terrible sounds. Then we hear a final scream, followed by a thud.)

VOICE. *(off) YYYYYYEEEEEEEEEAAAAAAAAAAAAAAAA!!!!!!!!*

(Thud!)

HOLMES. *He has beaten us, Watson!*

WATSON. *No, surely not!*

*(A **BODY** is lying prostrate amid the bushes, the head at a horrible, tell-tale angle. They are yards away, yet can see from the clothes that it's the body of **SIR HENRY**. Both **MEN** stop dead and gaze at him.)*

WATSON. *(grief-stricken)* ... Sir Henry. *He has killed Sir Henry! The brute! The brute!* When we find him, Holmes, I swear to you that I will put him away for life! Stapleton!

HOLMES. Stapleton. How dare he even *touch* my client! How dare he challenge me at my very own game! How dare he ... *I would have him drawn and quartered in the public marketplace!*

*(**WATSON** looks away, his face streaked with tears. **HOLMES** kneels at the body and starts to turn it over. At which point, **SIR HENRY** appears from the brush.)*

SIR HENRY. Holy cow. What happened here?

(seeing the body)

It looks like my cousin Daryl on a Friday night.

WATSON. *Ah! Sir Henry!*

SIR HENRY. What's the matter? Mr. Holmes!

WATSON. Sir Henry! Henry!

(**WATSON** *rushes over to him and is about to embrace him – then remembers that he's English and wrings his hand instead.*)

How good to see you! How marvelous!

(**HOLMES** *turns the body over.*)

HOLMES. Could this be … ? Ha ha! Yes it is! It's Victor, my some-time neighbor! The clothes! I'm a fool!

WATSON. Of course! The Barrymores gave Victor Sir Henry's old clothing to keep him warm!

HOLMES. Exactly! And the hound smelled the clothing.

SIR HENRY. What's goin' on?!

HOLMES. What's going on is that someone wants you killed, just as they killed Sir Charles before you.

SIR HENRY. But who could it be?

WATSON. I believe you'll find that Holmes –

(*Without* **SIR HENRY** *seeing it,* **HOLMES** *quickly puts his finger to his lips and shakes his head no.* **WATSON** *catches on and realizes that he's not to mention* **STAPLETON**'s *name.*)

– that Holmes is working on it, and he'll find out soon.

STAPLETON. (*off*) Hell-o! Anyone there!

SIR HENRY. It's Stapleton, the lyin' varmint. I wish he'd keep his nose out o' my business.

(**HOLMES** *pulls* **WATSON** *aside and whispers urgently:*)

HOLMES. Not a word to Sir Henry. We require his innocence or my plans crumble.

(*At which moment,* **STAPLETON** *enters. He looks as dapper and jaunty as ever.*)

STAPLETON. Ah, Doctor Watson, is that you? And who is – ?

(*He sees* **SIR HENRY** *and stops dead. His face goes white and he starts to stammer.*)

Sir – Sir Henry. I- I- I- what a – what a pleasure to see you again.

SIR HENRY. Likewise.

STAPLETON. I – I wouldn't have expected to meet you out here on the moors like this. And – and – is that a body? Oh my *dear.*

WATSON. It's Victor, the man who escaped from Princetown Prison.

STAPLETON. Oh dear me. And you must be Mr. Holmes, of course. We've been expecting you.

HOLMES. How do you do.

STAPLETON. Your exploits precede you, sir. Have you solved the mystery of Sir Charles's death?

HOLMES. I'm afraid I haven't, which is why I return so soon to London. I leave in the morning.

SIR HENRY. Hey, now hold it a second! You just got here!

HOLMES. Alas, Watson and I depart in defeat.

SIR HENRY. Watson, too? Then I lose a friend.

WATSON. I'm sure I'll be down again quite soon. And I trust you'll visit us in London.

MISS STAPLETON. *(off, calling)* Jack? Oh, Jack, you know I don't like being left out here on the –

(She enters looking beautiful but distressed. She sees **HENRY** *and her face lights up with relief and love.)*

Henry! What a wonderful surprise. What are you doing here?

SIR HENRY. I was out with my friends. You know Doctor Watson, of course. And this is Sherlock Holmes.

HOLMES. How do you do.

MISS STAPLETON. Mr. Holmes? Oh, what a pleasure. We've been expecting you for so long, and I'm so grateful, so pleased that you've come at last! *Oh, this could change everything!*

HOLMES. Why? Are you in distress, madam?

*(***STAPLETON** *looks up sharply. There is a tense pause.)*

STAPLETON. Why do you say that, Mr. Holmes?

HOLMES. *(with a smile)* Usually only those in distress are glad to see me.

STAPLETON. Hm? Oh. Ha! Ha ha! Ha ha ha ha ha ha! Very good, Mr. Holmes! The rest want to run away from you, eh? Hahahahahahahaha! Shall we still see you tonight for dinner then, Sir Henry?

SIR HENRY. Of course.

STAPLETON. Wonderful. 'Til then.

(STAPLETON heads off with MISS STAPLETON.)

SIR HENRY. *(to WATSON)* I'll go have the Barrymores pack up your things.

WATSON. Thank you.

(SIR HENRY exits. HOLMES lingers to talk to WATSON.)

HOLMES. What a nerve he has! He's as cool as one of his butterflies, tempting capture, then fluttering away. Let us pray we can stop him before his next kill. Now quickly, Watson, we have a train to meet.

(Thump, thump, thump, thump. Ominous music.)

(Whoooeee! A train whistle sounds as we arrive at:)

Scene Seven: The Platform of the Train Station at Coombe Tracy

CARTWRIGHT. Cartwright.

MILKER. And Milker.

CARTWRIGHT. Reporting for duty,

CARTWRIGHT/MILKER. *sir!*

HOLMES. Did the letter arrive at my residence?

CARTWRIGHT. Yes, sir.

MILKER. I got it.

CARTWRIGHT. We *both* got it!

(CARTWRIGHT hands the letter to HOLMES. HOLMES opens it and pulls out a photograph.)

HOLMES. Satisfactory. Indeed superlative. My next move is to visit Laura Lyons.

(**CARTWRIGHT** – *the actor* – *takes this in and dashes into the wings to change.*)

MILKER. We'll be in touch.

(*He exits.*)

WATSON. Tell me, Holmes. Why not arrest this blackguard at once? We know he's guilty.

HOLMES. Proof, proof! We have nothing against him! That's the cunning of it!

WATSON. There is Sir Charles's body.

HOLMES. Found dead without a single mark upon him. Of more importance, there's an absence of motive. Why would he do it?

WATSON. What do you propose?

HOLMES. I have great hopes of this Laura Lyons. Let us repair immediately to her typing establishment.

Scene Eight: Mrs. Laura Lyons' Typing Establishment

(**MRS. LYONS** *appears dramatically. She is distraught and put-upon, out of a melodrama.*)

MRS. LYONS. Yes! It was I who sent the letter to Sir Charles, it was I who begged him to help me, and it was I who asked him to meet me at the gate! But I never went to the meeting, I swear!

HOLMES. You're lying.

MRS. LYONS. *I am not!*

HOLMES. *Of course you are!* Now we regard this case as one of murder, and the evidence may implicate not only your friend Mr. Stapleton, but his *wife* as well.

(*It's as though* **HOLMES** *has dropped a bomb.*)

MRS. LYONS. His wife? ... *His wife?!* He's not a married man!

WATSON. I'm afraid he is.

MRS. LYONS. Prove it! Prove it to me!

HOLMES. *(taking the envelope that he received at the train station out of his breast pocket; he extracts the photograph; crisply)* I have here a photograph of the couple taken in York four years ago endorsed "Mr. and Mrs. Vandeleur," but you'll have no difficulty recognizing him. And his wife. I believe he pretends she's his sister, Beryl.

MRS. LYONS. ... He lied to me. He offered me marriage if I could get a divorce from my husband. He kept me from going to the gate to meet Sir Charles. The villain, the blackguard, *the evil man! HOW COULD HE!*

HOLMES. Madam, you have had a most fortunate escape. You had him in your power and he knew it. I suggest that *for your safety* you do not leave this room until tomorrow morning. Good afternoon.

WATSON. *(to MRS. LYONS, with sympathy)* Take care of yourself.

(Thump, thump, thump, thump. The music ratchets up the tension.)

HOLMES. *(to WATSON)* And now let us return to Baskerville. It is time to set the trap and spring it.

(Thump, thump, thump, thump.)

Scene Nine: Baskerville Hall: The Portrait Gallery

(HOLMES is giving instructions to SIR HENRY as WATSON listens. They're in the Portrait Gallery and the walls are lined with portraits of the Baskerville family.)

HOLMES. Sir Henry, you must do as I tell you, and do it blindly. I want you to drive to Merripit House for your dinner with the Stapletons, then send your carriage back and let them know that you intend to *walk* home.

SIR HENRY. Across the moor?

HOLMES. Exactly.

SIR HENRY. But that's what you keep tellin' me *not* to do.

WATSON. This time you may do it safely.

SIR HENRY. If that's what you tell me.

HOLMES. Good. Now call for the carriage or you'll be late for dinner.

SIR HENRY. If you say so, but I don't like it.

(He goes.)

WATSON. I must say, this is rather hard on poor Sir Henry.

HOLMES. Poor Sir Henry will thank us profusely if I can arrange to keep him ali –

*(**HOLMES** stops cold and stares at a portrait on the wall. It is one of the historic Baskervilles – though it is portrayed by one of our **ACTORS** – the one playing **STAPLETON** – with a frame around him. He is wearing the fancy costume of a 17th Century Cavalier, including the flowing hair, along with the beard, the moustache, the hat and the cloak. **HOLMES** is mesmerized.)*

WATSON. What is it? Holmes, what's the matter?

HOLMES. These portraits on the wall. They are, I take it, Sir Henry's ancestors?

WATSON. Yes.

HOLMES. And all of them Baskervilles?

WATSON. That's right. The one you're staring at is Sir Hugo, the one who started everything. Is something wrong?

*(**HOLMES** starts laughing gleefully.)*

HOLMES. Ha ha! Hahahaha! No, Watson, nothing is wrong. In fact something is very, very right at last. Ha! I'm aware that you think I know nothing of art, but I believe you'll agree this portrait remarkable.

WATSON. Well, I'd say it's very life-like, but I don't know that I'd call it "remarkable."

HOLMES. Oh I would, believe me. Step back a little. There. Now I want you to imagine the portrait without the hat …

(He takes the hat off the **ACTOR** *and tosses it aside.)*

without this heavy cloak he's wearing ...

(He removes the cloak.)

without all the hair ...

(He removes the wig and the beard.)

Now does it remind you of anyone?

WATSON. Good Lord! He looks like Stapleton!

*(**STAPLETON** stands tall and proud.)*

Same beady little eyes!

*(**STAPLETON** reacts.)*

Same weak, flabby chin.

(another reaction)

Same awful teeth.

*(**STAPLETON** is furious.)*

Good heavens!

HOLMES. Exactly. Good heavens. Praise heavens. Glorious heavens! Stapleton is a Baskerville! He must be the black sheep son –

WATSON. – of the brother who died in South America!

(They're so thrilled they almost dance.)

HOLMES. And there's our motive! The last piece of the puzzle! By killing Sir Henry, Stapleton stands to inherit everything. I should have seen it back at the Northumberland Hotel when we saw the Castilian Desk Clerk.

*(**STAPLETON** – the actor – steps forwards and transforms into the **DESK CLERK**:)*

DESK CLERK. To me it wath a mythtery from the bery beginning. The mithing boot, the mythterious letter, Meethter Sherlock Holmes – !

HOLMES. That's enough.

*(The **DESK CLERK** disappears; to **WATSON**:)*

Remind me to change hotels.

WATSON. Right. But how does Stapleton do it, Holmes? The creature is real – at least it seems to be real …

HOLMES. Oh I'm on to him, Watson. And by tonight he'll be fluttering in our net as helpless as one of his own butterflies. Ha! Let's head to the station and meet Lestrade.

Scene Ten: The Train Platform at Coombe Tracy

LESTRADE. *(stepping off the train from London)* Well? Anything good this time, or is it just some Maharaja's missin' knickers?

HOLMES. It's the biggest thing in years.

WATSON. Are you armed?

LESTRADE. Does a duck piss in a pond?

HOLMES. Thank you for such a vivid metaphor. Did you bring the warrant I asked for?

LESTRADE. Does a bear go into the woods and –

HOLMES. *Thank you.* I need someone to arrest the most *singular criminal mind* I have ever come across.

LESTRADE. Well, what are we waitin' for? Let's go get the bugger and slam 'im to rights!

HOLMES. Excellent. Now it's off to the moors! Come! Quickly!

Scene Eleven: The Moors

*(The whole soundscape changes as the wind whooshes across the barren moors. The mud emits a hissing sound, the sky is dark, and the shadows of enormous rocks dot the terrible landscape. In the distance, about a hundred yards away, we see lights in the windows of a solitary house. **HOLMES, WATSON** and **LESTRADE** come into sight.)*

LESTRADE. Not a very cheerful place, now is it, Holmes? Look there! I see lights!

WATSON. That's Merripit House where Stapleton lives. He has killed one man and is trapping another.

LESTRADE. He sounds like a slippery sort of character to me.

HOLMES. That is the understatement of your career, Lestrade. Now Sir Henry Baskerville is inside and he should be emerging any minute. He'll then be alone coming up the path and that's when Stapleton will try to kill him. We'll ambush from here.

LESTRADE. Ambush. I like the sound o' that!

HOLMES. Watson, you've been in the house. What are those latticed windows at the corner?

WATSON. That's the dining room, I think.

HOLMES. Can you creep forward and see what they're doing? But be careful. Stay very quiet. God help us if Stapleton gets wise to us. Now go!

(Silence. **WATSON** *creeps forward to inspect the house. We move forward towards the house with* **WATSON.** *All is quiet save the wind and the hissing.* **HOLMES** *and* **LESTRADE** *watch him breathlessly.)*

LESTRADE. *(loud)* I'll bet they're having their dinner, the lucky buggers!

HOLMES. *Be quiet!*

(We see **WATSON** *look in the window. Then, unexpectedly, the door opens and* **STAPLETON** *comes out.* **WATSON** *plasters himself against the side of the house.)*

STAPLETON. *(calling indoors)* I'll be right back! Just checking the furnace!

(He closes the door and looks around shiftily. We hear boots upon gravel as he creeps to an out-building. He looks around and takes out a key. We hear the key in the lock; we hear the door open with a creak; and from inside the out-building we hear a scuffling noise, like that of a huge beast wanting its supper. Rooof! Whooof! Grrrrr!

When the scuffling and growling grow too loud for comfort, **STAPLETON** *shuts the door, locks it and returns to the house – at which point* **WATSON** *hurries back to* **HOLMES** *and* **LESTRADE**.*)*

HOLMES. Well?!

LESTRADE. What happened?!

WATSON. Dog. Enormous dog. Inside that building. Awful. And I saw no sign of Miss Stapleton at the table.

LESTRADE. Oh lord love a duck! Look at that!

WATSON. What?!

LESTRADE. The fog! Look at the fog! It's like pea soup!

HOLMES. Oh, no!

(And now we see a dense fog rolling towards them. It obscures everything in its path.)

This is the one and only thing that could stop us!

LESTRADE. Just leave it to me! I'll get to higher ground and I'll holler if I see anything.

WATSON. Good idea.

HOLMES. Go! *Go!*

LESTRADE. I move like a cat.

*(**LESTRADE** skirmishes off.)*

HOLMES. Damn the fog. And damn Sir Henry for taking his time! Our success and even his life may depend upon his coming out before the fog obscures everything.

WATSON. Look! One of the lights went out!

(They peer intently at the house.)

HOLMES. Come on, come on …

WATSON. The fog's getting worse. I can hardly see the path now.

HOLMES. *Shhh!*

*(**HOLMES** cocks his head and listens. Then he falls to the ground, flat out, and claps his ear to the ground.)*

Wait. Listen. I think I hear him coming out.

(In the distance we hear the door opening and we see **SIR HENRY** *bidding goodnight to* **STAPLETON**.)*

SIR HENRY. *(in the distance)* Goodnight. And thank you again. Sleep well.

(The door closes behind him. **SIR HENRY** *begins to walk up the path through the moor. He glances over his shoulder, ill at ease.* **HOLMES** *and* **WATSON**, *at a distance, watch him intently. The music is building.)*

(Then we hear the key in the lock of the out-building, and then we hear the door creak open on its hinges.)

HOLMES. *Hsst!*

*(***HOLMES** *pulls out his gun and cocks it.)*

Look out! It's coming!

(We hear the patter of a dog's feet – then we hear the dog break into a run – then we hear its ferocious growl – and then it leaps!)

HOUND. *RWAAAAAAAAAHHHHHHHHHH!*

*(***HOLMES** *and* **WATSON** *raise their revolvers and fire together.)*

(Bang! Bang!)

(The hound gives a hideous howl and drops for a moment. Then it jumps up again and make a leap for **SIR HENRY**. *It hurls him to the ground and begins attacking his throat – at which instant* **HOLMES** *and* **WATSON** *empty their guns into the ravenous beast – Bang! Bang! Bang! Bang! – and it falls to the ground with a final howl.)*

WATSON. *Henry!*

HOLMES. *Sir Henry!*

WATSON. *Are you all right?! Henry?!*

(They shake him and he opens his eyes and gasps with life.)

SIR HENRY. I'm ... what *was* it? I can hardly *ahhhhh!*

(He sees the corpse of the hound next to him.)

WATSON. It's all right. It's dead.

SIR HENRY. That is one big dog!

HOLMES. *(touching the paint on the hound's fur)* And he's painted with phosphorus, which reflects the light. The poor beast was starved, I have no doubt.

SIR HENRY. But who could do such a thing? Was it Stapleton?

HOLMES. I'm afraid so, and now we must find him. You stay here. Watson, quick! Into the house!

Scene Twelve: Merripit House

*(**HOLMES** and **WATSON** burst through the door of Merripit House, their revolvers at the ready.)*

WATSON. Damn! No sign of him.

HOLMES. He must have heard the shots and run.

WATSON. He's not in the kitchen.

HOLMES. Wait! I hear something!

VOICE. *(off)* Mpfff! Mmmmfffppppfffttt!

LESTRADE. *(entering)* I hear it too.

VOICE. *(off)* Mppppfff! Mpppffff!

WATSON. I think it's upstairs.

*(**LESTRADE** runs in, gun drawn.)*

HOLMES. Quickly, Watson, Lestrade, before he gets away!

*(They race up the stairs, and in the room at the top they find **MISS STAPLETON**, half-naked, gagged and lashed to one of the ceiling beams.)*

WATSON. Miss Stapleton!

HOLMES. The brute!

WATSON. Take the shackles off!

LESTRADE. *(impressed with her looks)* How do you do? Lestrade here.

MISS STAPLETON. Is he safe?! Has he escaped?!

HOLMES. He cannot escape us, madam. We won't let him.

MISS STAPLETON. No, no! Not Jack! I mean *Henry! Is he safe?!! Has he escaped the hound?!!*

WATSON. He has.

MISS STAPLETON. Oh thank God! Oh, this villain! See how he's treated me!

(We see welts on her shoulder and back.)

But this is nothing! It's my mind and soul that he's tortured and defiled. I could endure it all, all the solitude and ill-usage, once I met Henry. If only he'll forgive me!

*(She weeps. **SIR HENRY** appears at the door.)*

SIR HENRY. Forgive you? I would forgive you anything.

MISS STAPLETON. Oh my darling!

(They embrace.)

LESTRADE. What about that bugger Stapleton? Where did he go?

SIR HENRY. That's what I wanna know, 'cause I'm gonna tar him and feather him!

MISS STAPLETON. I can tell you. There is only one place he could have fled. There is an old tin mine on an island in the heart of the Mire. It was there that he trained his hateful hound, and there also he created a refuge in case he was ever found out.

WATSON. But could he find it in the dark like this?

MISS STAPLETON. Yes. That is, he could have, but – oh!

SIR HENRY. Tell us!

MISS STAPLETON. Knowing what he had planned, this morning I ... I shifted all the markers that he uses to find his way in. I put them in circles, round and round, then down the hill to the deepest part of the Mire behind the –

STAPLETON. *(off)* AAAAAAAAHHHHHHHHHHHHH!

*(They all run to the window and look out and down. There, in the distance we see **STAPLETON** being sucked into the Mire. They all react with noises of disgust.)*

HOLMES, WATSON, MISS STAPLETON, SIR HENRY.
Yuchhhh! Oh. Ooo. Ulhhh.

STAPLETON. *AAAAAAAAAAAAHHHHHHHHHH!*

*(They react again, only this time **LESTRADE** is one of them.)*

ALL. *Yuchhhh! Oh. Ooo. Oh, man.*

*(Gulp. **STAPLETON** disappears into the mud.)*

MISS STAPLETON. *Oh, Henry!*

*(She buries her face and sobs on **SIR HENRY**'s chest.)*

*(The lights dim, and everyone disappears, save **WATSON**.)*

Scene Thirteen: 221B Baker Street

DOCTOR WATSON. *(to the audience)* The resolution of the case took its toll on Holmes, for he was continually troubled by the conflict he felt between the atrocious nature of the crimes he dealt with and the thrill he took in their investigation. The hound, he said, was deep in all of us, the part of our souls that is dark and troubling, and it took him time to come to grips with it all. For my part, I was anxious to understand all the details of what had occurred so that I could begin to chronicle his latest exploit – but it was a full month before I could get him to discuss the case, which he finally did on a Sunday afternoon when we were back at our flat in Baker Street.

*(**HOLMES** enters.)*

HOLMES. Stapleton was indeed the son of Roger Baskerville, and when he realized that only two persons intervened between him and the title, he decided to kill them both. He settled in Devonshire for that purpose, learned about the legend of the hound, and that is where his genius came in. He relied on the legend to create the real thing: he used a gigantic mastiff, hidden, painted, and starved to do his killing. His wife tried to warn Sir Henry with her letter and used the cut-outs to disguise her handwriting in case her husband ever saw it. Meanwhile, Stapleton stole Sir Henry's boot to give the hound the smell of the man, which told me instantly that there was a real dog involved. So I had my suspicions before you even left for Devonshire. The one red herring in all this was the convict Victor, who had nothing actually to do with the case but clouded my judgment for a while – which was unforgivable.

WATSON. As if in answer to Holmes's self-reproach, the doorbell rang at this very instant, and Henry and Miss Stapleton arrived to inform us that they were getting married as soon as the law allowed, and asking *me* to be their best man.

(*A shout of joy, a burst of confetti, and the mood lightens.*)

HOLMES. This calls for a celebration. Come, let's go to the opera. My box is free and the opera is *Falstaff.*

Scene Fourteen: A Box at Covent Garden

(*On the stage, we're in the final moments of Verdi's* Falstaff. **FALSTAFF** *himself is center stage, singing his heart out. The final fugue begins "Tutto nel mondo e burla" – "Everything in the world is a joke." Above, in the box, we see* **SIR HENRY, MISS STAPLETON, WATSON** *and* **HOLMES,** *sitting together. We can hear them talking, with the exciting music in the background.*)

MISS STAPLETON. We owe everything to the two of you, and we're very grateful.

WATSON. *(abashed, modest)* Just doing our job, that's all.

HOLMES. We're proud to have been of some small help in the matter. *(wistfully)* And it was a relief, however briefly, to have something worth fighting for, something to help one forget the everyday, humdrum routine of our mortal existence …

(At which moment, the music stops abruptly. HOLMES *jumps to his feet and turns to the stage to see* FALSTAFF, *who has an odd expression on his face.* FALSTAFF *lets out a gasp and stammers out:)*

FALSTAFF. Plot against Queen. Dynamite. *Arghhhhhhhhhhh!*

(He falls forward onto the stage and there's a knife sticking out of his back. A WOMAN *screams.)*

(KABOOOOOOOOOOOM!!!)

(A huge explosion rocks the entire opera house.)

HOLMES. Well, Watson.

WATSON. Yes, Holmes?

HOLMES. I believe the wheel has turned yet again – and now it's back to work!

(The final bars of the opera ring out thrillingly from the orchestra.)

(Blackout.)

End of Play

Appendix

Projection from Page 23:

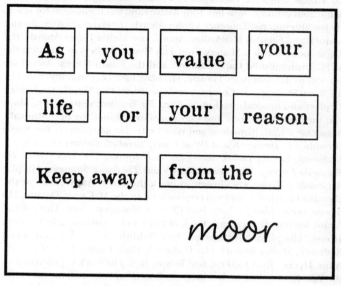

```
As   you   value   your

life  or  your  reason

Keep away   from the

            moor
```

Projection from Page 64:

Please, please, as you are a
gentleman, burn this letter,
and be at the gate by ten o'
clock. I feel so vulnerable.
                    LL

KEN LUDWIG has had six shows on Broadway and seven in London's West End, and his plays and musicals have been performed in more than 30 countries in over twenty languages. His first play on Broadway, *Lend Me A Tenor*, which the *Washington Post* called "one of the classic comedies of the 20th century," won two Tony Awards and was nominated for seven. He has also won two Laurence Olivier Awards (England's highest theater honor), the Charles MacArthur Award, two Helen Hayes Awards, the Edgar Award for Best Mystery from The Mystery Writers of America, the SETC Distinguished Career Award, and the Edwin Forrest Award for Services to the American Theatre. His plays have been commissioned by the Royal Shakespeare Company and the Bristol Old Vic. He has written 23 plays and musicals, including *Crazy For You* (five years on Broadway and the West End, Tony and Olivier Award Winner for Best Musical), *Moon Over Buffalo* (Broadway and West End), *The Adventures of Tom Sawyer* (Broadway), *Treasure Island* (West End), *Twentieth Century* (Broadway), *Baskerville, Leading Ladies, Shakespeare in Hollywood, The Game's Afoot, The Fox on the Fairway, The Three Musketeers* and *The Beaux' Stratagem*. His play *A Comedy of Tenors* was chosen to mark the 100th Anniversary of the Cleveland Playhouse and was co-produced by the McCarter Theatre. His newest book, *How To Teach Your Children Shakespeare*, won The Falstaff Award for Best Shakespeare Book of 2014 and is published by Random House. His plays have starred Alec Baldwin, Carol Burnett, Lynn Redgrave, Mickey Rooney, Hal Holbrook, Dixie Carter, Tony Shalhoub, Anne Heche, Joan Collins, and Kristin Bell. His work is published by the Yale Review, and he is a Sallie B. Goodman Fellow of the McCarter Theatre. He holds degrees from Harvard, where he studied music with Leonard Bernstein, Haverford College and Cambridge University. For more information, please visit www.kenludwig.com.